Taboo Erotica Short Stories Collection: Explicit Erotica For Adults- Orgasmic Oral, Gangbangs, Threesomes, Sex Games, Femdom, MILFs, Spanking, BDSM & More (Forbidden Fantasies Series)

© **Copyright 2021 - All rights reserved.**

The content contained within this book may not be reproduced, duplicated or transmitted without direct written permission from the author or the publisher.

Under no circumstances will any blame or legal responsibility be held against the publisher, or author, for any damages, reparation, or monetary loss due to the information contained within this book; either directly or indirectly.

Legal Notice:

This book is copyright protected. This book is only for personal use. You cannot amend, distribute, sell, use, quote or paraphrase any part, or the content within this book, without the consent of the author or publisher.

Disclaimer Notice:

Please note the information contained within this document is for educational and entertainment purposes only. All effort has been executed to present accurate, up to date, and reliable, complete information. No warranties of any kind are declared or implied. Readers acknowledge that the author is not engaging in the rendering of legal, financial, medical or professional advice.

Table of Contents

The Bar Milfs Wild Night 1

The Maid's Special Skill 24

Teacher's Pet 45

Best friend's Secret 66

Pleasing the Donors 88

The Forbidden Patient 109

Deeper than Mere Friendship 131

Her new Farmhands...153

The Billionaire's Secret..174

The Bar Milfs Wild Night

"Come on, one more drink," I said with a smile as I took the glass to my lips, sipping on the dregs of this. I let out a sigh of contentment at the fact that the liquor was hitting nice and deep.

"Come on Tiffany, aren't you like....getting to your limit?" Patricia asked.

I looked at her, laughing hard as I felt my eyes start to grow a bit dilated at this.

"What do you mean? I don't have a limit," I said to her.

She shrugged.

"Come on Tiffany, you know what happened the last time you were drinking way too much. Remember when you threw up everything?" she said.

I remembered that. It was a night of dumbass choices, and I definitely regretted it, however.,...she did have a point.

"Maybe you do have a point," I said, feeling the alcohol hit my head, but not to the point where I was blackout drunk. I just wanted to feel something you know.

It was the first night out since my divorce from Chad. I was so glad to finally be out of that shit.

Chad was the biggest fucking dickhead. He was an asshole, and he only cared about himself. I hated it, especially when I caught him sleeping with the coworker that he had. He claimed they were just friends.

Right. Just friends.

I filed for divorce immediately after. That was the straw that broke the camel's back, but now....I didn't know what to do.

"What the fuck," I said, slamming the drink down with a thud. I got up, stumbling for a second. Patricia got me, and I smiled at her.

"You need to be careful there," she said.

"I'm doing the best that I can," I told her.

It's weird because for me, alcohol either turns me into a fucking horndog, or made me into a total mess.

And tonight, I was horny as fuck.

My son was at his friend's house, so I had the night to myself. Well not just that, but of course I needed something a bit different.

I looked over at Patricia, who was already on her way to the way to the dance floor at the bar. I joined her moments after I got myself together, seeing that she was in the corner with a couple of guys.

College kids. Perfect.

I smiled, pushing my hair back and sauntering over to the two guys. They looked at us with surprise, unable to say anything.

"Yes?" one of the guys asked.

"Hey there. We saw you two looking pretty cute. Thought we'd come say hi," Patricia said.

"Yes. I was thinking the same thing. Can't believe they let cute guys like you tow out like this," I purred to them.

They blushed, and the one who seemed a little timider, a blonde guy with obvious muscles, blue eyes that looked downwards, and shapely, muscular legs, spoke.

"Yeah my buddy Gavin and I were just handing out here. I'm Mark by the way," he said.

"Tiffany. So cutie, what you guys doing tonight?" I asked them.

"Damn, already jumping into there," Patricia said, lightly elbowing me.

I smirked, enjoying the responses these two guys had. The awkwardness of the conversation was obvious, but I didn't care. I just enjoyed the fact that this was happening, and the way that they looked at me with nervousness.

"We were just going to come here and see if we could find anyone. Celebrating finishing our junior year of college," I heard Mark say.

"Amazing. I'm excited for you two," I replied.

3

Mark had dark hair, looked Italian, and had dark hazel eyes. He was cute, but Gavin the blonde was a lot more my type. He was a bit awkward, and there was something utterly cute about this.

I couldn't get enough of it.

I licked my lips, enjoying the way he simply looked at me, my curvy body enticing him.

"What's the matter?" I asked him.

"N-nothing just…you look good," the blonde said.

I flushed. I liked it when men gave me compliments. It was thrilling, and there was something about the way that they sounded that made me feel really excited, almost thrilled really, and it made me want to learn more about this too.

"Anyways, want to head somewhere else? Or dance a bit?" Patricia asked.

"I wouldn't mind dancing with a woman as pretty as you," Mark said.

She took his hand, moving over to the corner, and soon their bodies were against one another, gyrating, shaking around, and I couldn't help but want that too.

I looked over at Gavin, who was shuffling around, nervous as all hell at the way I looked at him. I pulled him closer, our bodies moving against one another.

Gavin was both confident, but also nervous as hell. He looked at me, blushing crimson as I smiled at him. He was tall, and his muscular arms felt nice.

"So you come here a lot?" I asked him as I moved my body around.

"Yeah, but usually alone. I'm always out here...looking for new people," he said to me.

"Well, I'm a new person, and I can certainly show you a great time," I purred.

"I'd...I'd like that," he said.

I moved closer, feeling the erection in his pants start to come to life. That's when it surprised me.

He was big. Much bigger than I expected him to be. I licked my lips, looking over at Patricia as we both had the plan in place.

The goal was to get two guys to come over to the room that we had, and enjoy a wild night together. It was something we'd been working to plan, but haven't really managed to find someone.

Until now what is.

I looked over at Gavin, who seemed to be getting uncomfortable. I leaned in closer, my lips near his ear.

"Want to go back to my place so we can have some fun?" I asked him. I imagined that's what he wanted to do.

He looked at me, his eyes wide with shock, but then nodded.

"Y-yeah. I'd like that," he said.

"Well then let's go. I have a room at the hotel next to the bar," I told him.

There was a really nice hotel nearby. When I took his hand, I could see the awkwardness that was there. But then, we walked on over to the room, stepping inside and going to the elevator. Patricia followed me, with Mark's hand in hers.

"Oh, he's coming too?" Gavin said.

"Yeah, I thought this may be a fun little experience for both of us. We can...enjoy ourselves together," I purred.

He groaned against me, and I enjoyed the way I teased this man. There was something fun about teasing him that was different from other guys. We got inside, and I soon moved to the bed, grabbing him and pulling him so that he was right over me.

He looked at me, awkwardly hovering his body over mine. I smirked.

"Is this your first time?" I asked.

I'd laugh if I ended up picking a virgin, but he shook his head.

"No just...first time with a woman as pretty as you. I lost it to this really ugly chick," he said.

"Aww that's a shame. Well I can make you forget," I said in his ear.

I pulled his face towards mine, looking him in the eyes. He was definitely a cutie, and it made me feel nice and young doing this. Before I could say anything else, our lips were on our own.

There was something hot about hearing Patricia next to me, making out with Mark. Mark seemed to be the type who was a little bit more open with his actions, and he wasn't as nervous. But I did admit, kissing Gavin was something amazing, and thrilling as well.

We started Marking out, enjoying the feeling of this, loving the feeling of one another as we continued to let our lips collide, our tongues move and dance. He was pretty good at kissing as well. I wondered if I'd get to experience Mark as well.

The way his lips felt so subtle turned me on. I then saw Gavin pull away, looking at me with a flush.

"You're good," he said.

"It's because I have over a decade of experience over you sweetie. And you will get to enjoy all of that tonight," I said.

I was happy to have this experience. I mean, I was married for almost 2 decades before I caught the rat bastard cheating. I'm glad that I was good enough to make this young man flush, enjoying the way that I teased him.

For a long time, we just made out, our bodies moving closer. I arched my hips slightly, enjoying the way that he moaned in response, moving his hips near mine. I

7

shuddered, shivering with a need that only grew more so as we continued to make out passionately. Gavin was definitely a looker, and he knew exactly how to kiss easily.

This younger man was already tearing me apart, turning me on in ways that I didn't think were even possible. I shivered, arching my back as he continued to pepper kisses there, our tongue moving together. I wanted him, and I definitely could tell that he wanted this too. But there was a nervousness there.

"Something the matter?" I finally asked as he pulled away.

"No. it's just…sorry I'm a little nervous. You're the first woman I've done it with that's been…really hot," he said to me.

I flushed, appreciating how he called me that. It was nice.

"I do appreciate it. I'm glad that you enjoy it," I told him.

"Boy do I," he said.

Our lips crashed together once again, loving the way that we felt against one another. It was definitely the thrill of the moment, the excitement of the future, the nature of this which made us both excited and turned on.

His lips moved downwards, touching my neck slightly. I shivered, looking over to see that Mark's hands were already at her clothes, tearing them off of her.

I don't know why, but there was something hot about seeing that. But then, I felt a little nibble against my neck, pulling me back to the feeling at hand.

Gavin was a little bit awkward with the way his hands touched. I shivered with delight, enjoying the way his hands barely grazed against my breasts. I could feel his hands touching in curiosity, exploring me.

"You can touch all you want," I told him.

"O-okay," he said.

He reached up, grabbing my breasts and teasing them there. I shivered, moaning in pleasure as I enjoyed this. His hands became exploratory, and I loved how they danced against my nipples.

I made quick work of my shirt, pulling it off. I pressed his face between my chest, touching his face there against the breasts.

"They're so...warm," he said, muffling them there.

"They are. And I'm sure you'll enjoy them," I said.

My breasts got a lot bigger after having my son, but I wasn't against that. I know that my husband liked them before he decided to be a cheating asshole, and I could see from the look on his face, the excitement in his eyes, and the obvious hardness in his pants, he enjoyed this too.

He moved his hands downwards, touching the nipple and playing with it there, teasing it against his hand. I let out a small gasp, enjoying the feeling of his hand there.

This guy, despite being inexperienced as fuck, was a lot of fun to fuck around with, and I enjoyed it a whole lot. He soon moved his hands towards the tip of my nipples, touching them there through the fabric, making me shiver and cry out with delight, moving my hips upwards.

His hands moved to the back of my bra, touching the clasp there. I looked at him, seeing the struggle in his eyes, but then I laughed.

"Let me help you out," I told him.

I pulled off the bra, tossing the garment over to the side. I looked at him, smiling with a coy grin as he looked at me, his eyes wide with surprise.

"Wow," he said.

"You can touch them," I told him.

He quickly moved closer, refusing to say no to that offer. He took the tip of the nipple into his mouth, sucking on the flesh there. I let out a small moan, excitement growing within me as he pushed it between his lips, enjoying the sounds that I made. I shivered with delight, enjoying the way he continued to tease and play with it. His lips were soft, exploratory, and I noticed another set of fingers move upwards, teasing the nipple there. I cried out as he did this, thrusting m y hips upwards, enjoying the feeling of this.

He continued to play and tease around with them, and I let out a small moan, excited about this. His hands and lips worked their magic, and I enjoyed the sensation of this as well.

I continued to move my hips upwards, enjoying the little pinches that he did with his fingers. Mark was already between Patricia's legs, expertly eating her out. She let out a series of cries, and there was something about this that I found hot, that I enjoyed, and that I wanted to hear more out of.

But then, he pulled on both of the nipples, tugging on them, making me shiver with delight, enjoying the feeling of this. I shivered, loving how easily I was losing all semblance of control, all because of this man, and his expert hands.

Even though he wasn't that experienced, I'd be lying if I said I didn't enjoy it. But then, he slithered his fingers downwards, against my body, pushing his hands towards my pants. He touched my thighs, feeling the large muscles there, and I chuckled.

"You like?" I teased.

"Yes. Very much so," he purred.

"Good. Because I like this too," I said to him.

He then moved his hands to the jeans, pulling them slightly. He tried to tug them off, but there was no dice. My butt was a little too big for that one. I pushed my hips up, meeting his cock and letting out a small groan as he pushed it off of him, looking at me, seeing the look of pure need which was there on my face.

"Fuck," he said, taking a moment to drink me up. I knew I was needy. I hadn't been fucked hard in a moment, and I knew that his monstrous dick would do the job.

"Like it?" I said.

"Yes," he replied with a gulp.

I moved my hands downwards, spreading apart, but then, he moved his hands gingerly against my thighs, trailing little touches upwards till he got to the apex of my legs. He inhaled for a second, letting out a sigh of contentment before he pulled off my panties, revealing my shaven, wet pussy.

He looked at it, surprised by this.

"It's so fluffy," he said.

"Like it?" I asked him.

"Yes," he replied.

He moved his hands down between there, exploring me slightly. He then pressed against my clit, making me shiver and cry out with delight, pushing my hips upwards as I felt his hands explore and touch every single part of me. His hands moved towards the tip of my clit, pressing there, watching my eyes widen with surprise at the soft, sensual touches there. He rubbed me there, enjoying the sounds of my desire, the pleasure that came from this, and the aching need.

He was good. He then moved a finger inside, exploring my entrance, looking at me with a look of curiosity and desire.

"Fuck," I said out loud.

"You...good?" he asked me.

"Yeah. Amazing," I told him.

He continued the exploratory touches, pumping his fingers in and out, watching with rapt desire as I continued to move my hips slightly, thrusting upwards and enjoying this. I watched his eyes grow heavy with lust, and then, he spread me apart, pushing his tongue inside, digging into me.

I cried out, surprised by just how needy this man was, and the touches that he provided to me. Everything just felt so...amazing really. It was a thrill that I couldn't get enough of, something that I just felt that I needed more than anything else. I continued to press my hips upwards, pushing my hands to his face, smothering him with my pussy.

I heard the muffled gasps and sounds, but his tongue continued to work its magic, invading inside of me, moving upwards to tease my clit, and it got me so close that I thought I'd lose control for a moment. But then I stopped myself, looking over at him with a devilish grin.

"You good?" I asked him with a smile.

"Yeah," he replied.

"Anyways, I guess you enjoyed that," I told him.

"You didn't...cum did you?" he asked.

"God no. going to take more than that," I teased.

He flushed, but then nodded. However, I reached out, touching the obvious outline in his pants.

13

"Let's have a look at this, shall we?" I asked.

I slid his pants down, revealing his cock. He was big, much bigger than I imagined, and he was already leaking out precum. He was girthy too, and I licked my lips, excited for the taste of this, and so much more. I moved my lips to the tip, kissing and tasting the precum that was there, seeing his eyes grow heavy with need.

"You good?" I asked him.

"Yeah," he replied.

I smiled, seeing him struggle to hold onto this, all semblance of control taking him to a whole new place. I then moved my lips to the tip, sucking on this, watching him groan in pleasure, pushing his hips upwards, moaning in excitement and surprise.

He then started to press my had there as I took him further and further in. He grabbed my hair, holding it as he began to fuck my face. I felt the tears begin to fill in my eyes, but I held steady, taking his cock in deeper and deeper, mustering every ounce of strength not to pull back.

I got to the base before I could feel the urge to gag. I then pulled back, licking the underside of his cock. He pushed me back down again, thrusting his hips upwards, and I shivered, enjoying the delightful sensation of this. There was something fun about being used just like this, and I could tell from the way he continued to do this that he was enjoying this just as much as I was.

But then, as soon as it happened, he pulled back, smiling at me with excitement.

"You good?" he said.

"Yes. Now just fuck me," I said.

I moved down, spreading my legs apart, watching in anticipation as he groaned. He then pushed his legs towards me, spreading me apart, and then, he slid himself deep into me.

To my surprise, he fit pretty well in there, almost too well. I suddenly let out a small cry, surprised by how good this was as he continued to thrust in deep, and I let out a series of cries, enjoying the pleasure that came from this.

Every single touch, every single caress, it was all driving me to the point of madness. His cock filled me right the fuck up, pushing out, then pushing in, enjoying the tightness of my pussy.

"Yes, just like that," I said. He continued to press deep, hitting so hard that I didn't know how much more of this I could take.

That's when I got an idea.

I heard the sound of groaning and crying from someone. I looked over, seeing Patricia there, getting pounded into the bed by Mark. He was pretty big too, but of course, Gavin was bigger.

"Get me from behind," I said.

15

"Are you...sure?" he asked.

"Yes, I love it," I told him.

I moved myself on all fours, shaking my butt. He then groaned, grabbing my cheeks and pushing himself into me. The sheer force of his thrust as he filled me up made my eyes start to widen, and I felt the urge to salivate right then and there. He continued to thrust in deep, pushing me to my limits as I let out a small cry, holding onto the sheets. Patricia looked at me, smiling.

"This is one hell of a way to celebrate you getting divorced," she said.

"Sure as shit is," I told her.

I then moved in, pressing my lips to hers, and as we both got pounded by these two, we made out, our tongues moving and touching against one another. There was something super thrilling about this, and I couldn't get enough of this. But then, we pulled back, as I felt him hit that one spot, the location that always made me whimper, becoming a puddle of goo right then and there.

"Holy shit," I cried out, feeling my back arch. He grabbed my hair, pounding me harder and harder. A hand was on my ass, and another hand touched my pucker, teasing it.

I groaned, feeling that need, that urge for two dicks inside of me. Before I knew it, Patricia let out a cry, passing out.

"Fuck," she said to herself.

"You okay?" I asked her.

"Finish them off," she told me.

I knew what they meant. I looked over at Mark, moving off.

"Want to go behind?" I said.

"Sure," he said.

I got myself on top of Gavin, holding onto him as I shifted my weight down, feeling his cock all the way inside of me as I let out a small, garbled scream as he penetrated me deep. I couldn't get enough of this, and I knew that he was enjoying this as much as I was.

But then, I felt something against my other entrance. At first, it was a finger, and that combined with the cock in my other hole, was already driving me crazy. He pushed himself all the way in, and I cried out, feeling him penetrate me completely with it. But then, Marks' cock replaced the fingers which were teasing me for a bit, and I suddenly let out a small, subtle cry.

"Yes," I shivered, moaning out loud as I felt it get deeper and deeper inside of me. There was a tightness, something which was common when I got that entrance pounded. But then, he was all the way inside of me. I shivered, enjoying the tightness and the fullness which came from this.

I started moving slightly, enjoying the feeling of this. But then I felt Gavin hold onto me, keeping me between them as they both began to thrust their cocks deep into me. I started to shiver with delight, enjoying me as I pushed against them, feeling their cocks penetrate my body deeply.

They thrust in harder, causing me to tense up. I enjoyed this, religion in the feeling of everything as I felt them both continue the onslaught on my holes, holding me there as they thrust in deep.

I was so close. I felt like I was about to reach my limit. Then, I felt Gavin pull me forward, looking me in the eyes.

Then, our lips met. We kissed, and he angled my hips slightly, pressing right up against the g-spot. That, combined with the location of where Marks's thrusts were hitting made me get so close that I could taste it. And I felt a small hand move downwards, teasing my clit as I tensed up, shivering as I cried out loud, thrusting my hips upwards as I came hard.

By that point, when my tight pussy and ass clenched onto them, that was more than enough for them. Mark was the first, groaning as he shot his load into my ass.

But then, Gavin pulled out, grabbing his cock, and then shoved it right in my face. Spurts of cum decorated my face, and I stuck out my tongue, drinking the rest of it as it fell from his member.

I looked at him, giving him a small, wry smile as I saw him sit back, moaning out loud.

"Holy. Shit," he said.

"You good there?" I asked him.

"Yeah. Utterly amazing really. I just don't know what else to say. Other than…wow," he said.

I chuckled, leaning in, giving him a small kiss on the lips. I then pulled back, nodding.

"Don't you worry. We'll have more fun times like this down the road," I said to him.

There was an excitement that made me feel good about all of this. I loved the fact that he was enjoying this as much as I was. He then pulled back, sighing.

"Well shit," he said.

"Yeah, that's right. And I guess you knocked out Patricia. I knew that she wasn't the type to last long in bed, but damn," I said.

Patricia gave me the middle finger.

"I heard that."

"Sure you did," I retorted.

We all laughed, feeling the excitement and thrill of the moment begin to die down. I didn't know what else to say next, but then, I saw that Mark was looking around nervously.

"What's the matter?" I asked him.

"Well it's just….I didn't expect to have this happen tonight. Thought we'd pick up some younger girl," he said.

"What, is my old ass not enough for you?" I teased.

"Not at all! It's just...surprising," he said to me.

"Well, I enjoy this. And I'm glad that I can make you guys pretty happy too," I told them.

They all nodded, agreeing to my words. But then, Gavin spoke.

"Yeah, I'm definitely happy with the way things are going. Thanks for making things fun," he said to me.

"You're most welcome. I love having fun," I told him.

"Me too," Gavin replied.

"Anyways, you guys want to spend the night or..."

Mark and Gavin both shook their heads.

"Actually, we do need to be back at the dorms tonight," Gavin said.

"Yeah, we can't stay out too late or also the DA will get mad at us again," Mark replied.

So they were the type that snuck out after hours. What a bunch of naughty boys. My lips curled into that of a smile as I pushed my brown hair back, my green eyes scanning over the two of them. They were both a snack and then some, but I also was a bit surprised by the results of this too.

"That's totally fine. You two be safe though, you hear?" I asked them.

"Yeah, we will be. Thank you...Tiffany," Gavin said.

"Yeah, it was fun," Mark replied.

I watched as they got out of the doorway, closing it. I walked over to lock it. When I turned around, Patricia had come back to reality. I guess that dick really did do her some good.

"Everything alright?" I asked her.

"Yeah. Just was surprised at how fucking good that dick was," she said.

"Me too. Oh and by the way, you looked really hot there. I don't know, I wanted to kiss you because of it," I admitted, flushing red.

I don't know why, but there was something enticing about saying those words., she simply beamed, and I wondered if this was something she was all for or not.

"Really now?" she said.

"Yeah, I'm really glad that...we could enjoy that together," I told her.

"Well I'm glad that we could too," she replied.

I leaned in, giving her a hug, and we kissed again. It was a strange platonic friendship. I didn't want anything romantic with Patricia at all, but being with her, kissing her, all of this just felt...so damn good you know?

"Anyways, I think it's getting late. We should probably get some sleep. Unless...you want to go back down and do the same thing once again," she said.

I was surprised by Patricia. Sure that dick was good, but it'd be fun to try things out with another guy. To enjoy the thrill of more sex, the dick, and to have this again and again.

"Sure, I wouldn't mind that. Let me go take a shower. I kind of have cum all over my face you know," I said.

She laughed.

"Yeah he really got you," she said.

I went to the bathroom to freshen up, but it was nice to finally have the freedom that I'd been waiting for. My husband never let me have some time like this with the girls, even if there wasn't sex involved. But now, I got to experience this again and again, and I loved everything about it. It certainly was the beginning of a new life for me.

Maybe the singles life wasn't all that bad, you know?

I came on back, smiling warmly to Patricia, who was in a whole new outfit. I got my own outfit too. The night was young, and there were still some super-hot guys around. I had a feeling that Mark and Gavin were already gone, so we can go out once more.

"You ready?" Patricia asked.

"Give me just a moment," I said.

I stood in the mirror, putting on makeup and smiling as I looked in the mirror. I felt hot, hotter than I'd been in the last few marriages that I had, and a whole lot hotter than I thought.

22

It was time to go down again, to have some fun, get into more mischief, and of course, to explore the fun that would come out of this, and not just that, the adventures that we'd been waiting for, and the thrill of the next cutie that would come my way, just begging to give me his cock.

The Maid's Special Skill

I needed a job, and this was the first one that I'd managed to nab.

It was working for a mysterious gentleman. A guy named Gregory Kifman, some big-time dude who lived in a big mansion.

I was employed to work as his maid, and at first, we didn't have any contact with one another. Hell, I literally had an interview over the phone. It was so weird. I'd never experienced anything like this before.

I figured I'd end up losing the job or something to some other girl who probably sounded like a sex worker. But no....I got the job.

I was told to meet up on Monday, and so I did. When I got there, the place was practically empty, save for one red car. Did he have any other special hands.

"Is this the right place?" I asked myself. It had to be. This was what I found on Maps, and it was the right address. When I got to the door, I realized there was an intercom. I pressed it.

"Yes," the voice said curtly.

"Hi there. I'm Amanda. I'm here for the new job," I explained.

I hoped that this would work, that I wouldn't get into deep trouble because of this. But then, he spoke.

"I see that you're here," he told me.

"Yeah. Sorry about that," I told him.

"Very well. Give me a few moments," he said to me.

I looked around, trying to keep my wits about me. He probably was just some grumpy old man who probably acted like he was better than everyone else because he was an old man who had money.

But then, the door opened, and one of the most attractive men that I'd ever seen was in front of me. He had dark jet-black hair, dark blue eyes that looked unreal, and he was both small, but also had a defining build to him.

I suddenly licked my lips on instinct, but then pulled myself back to reality. The last thing I wanted was to come off like a total dumbass.

"Oh, there you are. The new maid I hired, correct?" he said.

"Yes. Amanda," I replied.

He extended his hand and I took it, almost letting out a small moan as I felt his larger hand in mine. I shivered, enjoying the feeling of this, but I knew for a fact that it was only a matter of time before I'd just up and lose it right then and there. But then, he simply laughed.

"No need to be so formal. Come with me," he implored.

25

I followed him, the gears in my head spinning as I tried to figure out what the hell to do next. He motioned for me to sit at the table, and there was a maid dress and a whole piece of paper.

"There you go. That's all you need," he said.

"But aren't you going to go over the job and shit?" I asked.

I'd never experienced a guy like him. He shrugged.

"What else is there to go over. I can assure you, everything's there," he said to me.

I didn't know if he was just fucking with me, or not. Maybe he was, maybe I was overthinking all of this. But I read over the papers, and at that point, he was gone.

I didn't know why, but he both annoyed me, and it turned me on how cold he was. Maybe I had a thing for someone like that. I quickly pored over the notes of this, nodding.

"I see," I said to myself.

It was a pretty simple job. Just to clean the common rooms, and to not drop anything. I read that one plate in this place was worth more than my apartment's rent for the month! I hated that there were so many factors here, and so many extra things added, but also...this was the best job that I'd gotten.

I wanted to get to know Gregory. He was a bit quiet, and a little cold. But he was gone, vanished without a trace. It frustrated me that he did that, that's for sure. I wanted to get to know him, to find out more about him, but he was gone, and I guess I was destined to suffer at this point.

But I did what I needed to do. I decided at this point to get started with the tasks. I went to the bathroom to put the maid uniform on, and I realized that it was...kind of short, and it showed off my supple breasts. I pulled my red hair back, and I blushed a little at how I looked.

I thought I was pretty.

I quickly got myself together, heading back out. But as soon as I did, I bumped right into Gregory, who looked at me with a smile, sizing me up and down. His eyes did glaze down at the obvious chest I had in this, and I couldn't help but flush, but also felt turned on by how he looked at me.

"Very nice. Glad that it fits you," he said to me.

"Yes of course," I told him.

He looked me in the eyes, a look of purely heated desire there. I wasn't going to lie, I did think he was attractive, and he could do so many things to me and I'd live for every moment of it. There was something that just...pushed me to my limit, making me shiver and ache with both need and delight, the pleasure and lust growing within me.

"Yes, anyway, I'll let you get started with your work. I have a lot going on," he said to me, giving me one last look before heading on out of there.

My head was spinning. I couldn't help but feel the excitement and need grow within me.

I could see his eyes roving over my body, studying me with a look of pure need, want, and desire. I ached for this. And I felt my pussy wetten with delight at the sight of him.

Maybe it really was what I wanted.

But the duty called. I had to make sure that I took care of the surroundings, cleaning them as quickly as I could. I started in the main areas, working my way through the kitchen.

All the meanwhile I kept seeing his eyes glaze over my body, practically mentally undressing me as I looked into his eyes. There was something just so damn hot about this, and it made me shiver with delight, ache for him, and want him as he continued to study me, seeing the look of need as he was there.

Over the next couple of days, I did just this. I came in, I worked, I saw him mentally undressing me, which I smiled at, and then I'd leave. However, a couple of times I moved to the bathroom, pulling my skirt upwards, sticking two fingers into me, shoving them in. I let out a series of small little sounds, cries of need and want, aching for him as I continued to move my hands in and out, shivering with need as I continued to feel the urge and desire grow.

There was something just so fun about all of this, that I couldn't help but want this, need this, and desire everything that came from this.

I continued to engage in these tasks, moving around, trying my best not to be seen by him. but one time, I was in the bathroom, pushing my hand against my breasts, teasing my nipples through the confines of this shirt, when suddenly, I heard a knock at the door.

"Amanda?" Gregory asked.

I let out a small gasp, which I bit back before I quickly got my bearings together, getting fixed up before heading back over to the doorway. When I opened it, he was there, a frown on his face.

"What's the matter?" he asked.

"Oh nothing. Sorry I was taking so long. I was...attending to something," I said.

"I see. Well, I hope the cleaning gets done relatively quickly. If you need help with anything, please don't hesitate to ask," he said.

I looked at him, wondering if he meant something else there when it came to helping. I tried to hold back from licking my lips, the idea of his hands on my body, helping me as I helped him becoming a common image in my mind.

"Right. I'll definitely let you know then," I told him.

He smiled at me, and I could tell there was definitely something else going on there. I shivered, wondering if he would say anything more.

I went over to the kitchen to clean a couple of things. But what I didn't notice, was the wet floor that was there. As soon as I moved, I fell forward, slipping and hitting the side of the cabinet. Sure it fucking hurt, but there was something which worried me more.

The glass that was there.

It wobbled around, as if trying to test me, when suddenly there was a clang, and suddenly the glass fell down, shattering on the ground.

I paused, trying to figure out what the hell to do next. I was torn. I had no clue what to do here, or even what to say. Suddenly, I heard the pattering of footsteps, and I saw Gregory come in, a panicked look on his face.

"What the hell did you do?" he said, his face contorted into that of displeasure.

Shit, I was totally going to get fired. This wasn't good.

"I'm sorry, the floor was wet and—"

"And? You do know how much those glasses cost, right? You can't just run in here, slip on this, and expect me to just let this shit slide Amanda," he said.

I felt scared. Was I getting fired next? Would he just say screw it and kick mem out? This was the easiest job that I've had, and now, I may end up losing it because of a fuckup that made me feel abashed.

30

"I told you I'm sorry," I told him.

He pursed his lips, looking at me with disdain in his eyes.

"Well, this is a problem. I can't be having a maid who does this," he said to me.

I didn't know what to do. It was like life was fucking with me, making me want to just hide away, die and forget about it all.

In fact, it felt like I was making the biggest goddamn mistake of my life.

But I had to persist, right? I had to make this work. Suddenly, I tried to weigh my options.

I could beg for him to just let me go. To let my pathetic ass slide. But I didn't think that was going to work here.

There was another option. I knew he wouldn't take any shit from anyone, so maybe there was a chance for this to work.

I moved forward, pressing my chest upwards, a sorrowful look on my face.

"I could pay...another way," I offered.

He looked at me, at first his face a little bit confused. But then, he spoke.

"And how do you suppose you'll do that? What could you possibly offer to me?" he said.

I didn't want to have to do this, but it was the only thing that I could do. It was the only thing that would work in this case.

I started to move closer, my hand right up against the tip of his cock. I touched it through the outline of his pants, and he showed no emotion sans biting his lip.

"What are you doing?" he snapped.

"Helping you out. Wouldn't you like that?" I purred.

He tensed, but then nodded.

"Maybe I would," he said.

"Well, tell you what, I can let you have your fun with me, and we can call this a little misunderstanding," I told him.

He looked into my eyes, pursing his lips and tensing up, unsure of what to do, or what to say anymore. Finally, he spoke.

"Very well," he said, but there was clearly the sound of desire in his voice, as I continued to touch him there.

It was very obvious that he was turned on, and he definitely hadn't had this much in a long time. But then, I wondered what else he'd do.

As I was about to take his cock out of his pants, he pulled me upwards, looking at him.

"Not here. I need to punish you first," he said.

I looked at him, feeling a bit nervous about this. I wondered what he'd do. But then, he pulled me up,

32

practically dragging me to a room upstairs. It was probably his bedroom.

I hadn't been up in his bedroom as of yet, but when I got up there, I saw the beautiful sight. It was a nice space, and I was a little jealous of how nice it was. He then pushed me down on the bed, hoisting my skirt up, and rubbing his hand against my ass.

"You've got a cute little ass back here," he said to me.

I shivered, moaning with delight as he barely touched my pussy. He was such a tease, letting his hands rest there, and then move back to my backside. I felt his hand near my pucker too, and I tensed up.

I'd never been fucked there. What did he have planned for more.

Suddenly, before I could say anything more, he then pulled my panties down, revealing my bare ass.

"Damn," he said, grabbing it hard, holding it there. I let out a small grunt of surprise and pleasure, enjoying the way that this man touched me. There was something thrilling about the way his hands moved against there, rubbing my ass, touching it, teasing it, and enjoying it as well.

He continued to paw it, and then, he slapped it.

The slapping sensation was definitely amazing, and there was a thrill that came from this. I enjoyed it, that's for sure, and I knew that he liked it too. He started to smack me again and again, enjoying the way that I responded, and soon, I started tensing up, moaning in pleasure as he continued to smack me again and again, enjoying the feeling of all of this.

Everything was just so nice. It was perfect, a heavenly sensation that only made me ache for more. He continued to hit me harder and harder, enjoying the feeling of this, and I couldn't help but love everything about this too.

It was nice, that's for sure, and it was like he knew exactly how to touch me, how to make me feel good, and how to turn me on.

He then hit me harder, touching that one spot. As he smacked me, I shivered, crying out loud and tensing up.

"Look at you. Such a goddamn mess," he said to me, hitting me once again.

I cried out, arching my back, enjoying the feeling of this. His hands were tough, hardened, and there was something just so damn thrilling about him continually touching me, making me into the mess that I was.

With every single spanking, I felt my ass grow redder, and it felt a little bit tender. It definitely was getting me aroused, making me shiver with delight, enjoying the sensation of this.

But then, he stopped. I looked over, but he pushed my head down hard.

"I never said that we were done," he said.

I let out a small moan as he said those words. The power, the control, it was all making me shiver, the thirst that I had being quenched by the feeling of his body, and the tension that he created. Before I knew it, he soon grabbed something else, and when he hit me, a sting of pleasure hit my body, making me writhe with delight.

"Fuck," I cried out, shivering as he continued to hit me with the flogger. Every single touch was turning me on, driving me crazy, making me wish for more of this. I craved his touch. I needed it, and I could sense from the way that he did this to me that it was only making me ache for more. I definitely enjoyed this as well.

He continued the flogging, each lashing hitting my core. He got right by my pussy, and the vibration that I felt from the spanking touched every fiber of my being, making me ache for him, making me want more, and I needed this more and more.

I didn't know how much more of this I could take.

After a few more hits, he then stepped away. I didn't know what he had planned for me next. He then rubbed my ass, hitting it while I had my guard down, creating a garbled sound that came out of my mouth.

"You little shit. Over here breaking my stuff like this. Maybe I should make you pay with your body," he said to me.

In a way, the sound of that turned me on. I mean, if he kept me around for that, I'd stay forever. The way his hands continued to touch me, moving between my legs, teasing my clit, rubbing there, made me let out a garbled sensation, causing me to ache and moan in pleasure and need.

"Fuck," I shivered, crying out loud as things started to get even hotter for me. I was turned on, and I knew for a fact that he enjoyed this too.

After a few more moments, I suddenly felt like he was turning me on, and driving me crazy. He then pulled back, licking his fingers, but then he pulled me upwards, so that I was right by his cock.

"Take care of this," he grunted.

The sound of his voice reverberated through the core of my body. I quickly moved to his pants, undoing them, sliding them downwards, grabbing his cock as I touched it. He let out a small groan as I pushed it against my mouth, opening it as I started sucking on his cock.

I took the tip of it at first, watching his eyes grow wide as I sucked on the tip of it, hearing the small gasps as I continued to move my lips there, teasing the very tip of this. The sounds that he made were delightful.

Even though he was the one in control, I very much felt great about making him utter these sounds, delightful little utterances that were a turn-on to hear. I wanted to hear these again and again as I continued to move my lips around, sucking on the very tip of his cock, enjoying the sounds that came out of his mouth.

With every single touch, every single press, I was losing all semblance of control. It was driving me crazy, making me feel turned on, enjoying the feeling of all of this as he continued to groan.

The sounds that he made, the approval that was uttered, was something I couldn't get enough of. I loved hearing this, and every single time he groaned, moving his hips forward, I could tell that he liked this more and more.

I slowly pressed my tongue a little bit further down, moving towards the very tip of his cock, getting to the base and holding onto it there. He let out a small, garbled sound as I started to suck on the very base of his cock, hearing the utterances of approval that came from this.

The secret that I did have, was that I was great at sucking cock. I knew just what he wanted, the sounds that he uttered, the enjoying feelings that came out of this, it was all just...so damn perfect you know?

I continued to suck on him, getting to the very base of this, moving upwards, and he held my head there, forcing me to take it all the way down.

"There you go. Take all of this," he instructed.

"I'd do as I was told, pushing my head downwards, taking his load in my mouth if it did happen. I grabbed his cock, jerking it while I used my tongue, teasing every fiber of this, watching his eyes widen, and his cock start to jerk forward.

"Fuck," he said.

He pressed my head down, practically forcing me to take him to the very core. I did as I was told, sucking on him, holding him there as he continued to fuck my throat. I at this point was numb to everything, enjoying the feeling of all of this, and it was then when, after a few more moments, he suddenly kept my head down, but then pulled it back, shooting his load into my mouth, and partially onto my face.

His cum tasted way better than I expected, and I swallowed all of this, looking at him.

"You good?" I asked him.

"Yes. Great actually," he said.

But then, his hands moved to the back of my butt. I let out a gasp as he teased my pucker, encircling the edge, moving against the ring of muscles.

"But, I'm not done yet. You haven't fully paid it back. How about...I touch this part too," he purred.

My ass. He wanted my ass. In a strange way, I kind of liked it, and there was a thrill of being touched like this. I loved it, and soon, I felt my body slowly come apart, the need for him growing.

He reached over to his desk, grabbing what seemed to be lube out. He coated his fingers with it, smiling in excitement as he started to press the first digit into me. I suddenly cried out, feeling the ache of need grow within me. He then pushed his fingers into me, pressing two of them inside, and I cried out, tensing up as I felt this.

38

It was...different from what I thought. I definitely enjoyed this as much as he did, and with the way his fingers danced around, fingering my ass, pushing it to relax, it turned me on.

But I wanted something bigger in there. I wanted his fingers all the way inside me. He then added another finger, pushing deep within, and as he continued to fuck me, I felt the sudden discomfort turn into that of pleasure.

This was amazing. It was a turnon that only made me ache for more.

After a few more thrusts, he then pulled back, groaning once again. I figured he was hard. He then pushed the tip of himself inside, filling me up completely, making me shiver and ache with desire as he continued to push all the way in.

He was bigger than I expected. Sure I did just suck his cock, but that was different from well...having it all the way in there. I suddenly cried out, pushing forward, enjoying the sensation of this as he continued to press himself into me, turned on by the feeling of me against him. This was thrilling, a different type of feeling compared to what I was used to.

When he was all the way inside, he stopped, smacking my ass as I cried out, feeling the tightness become almost suffocating as he moved his hands to my hips, holding them there.

Then he thrust. When he did so, it touched a part of me that I thought I'd never get to feel. I cried out, suddenly aching for more, the encroaching need for him growing more and more. He continued to thrust in and out of me, each touch of this turning me on, and there was something exciting, thrilling, and needing about all of this. With every single thrust too, he smacked my ass, so I could feel him continuously tease me.

A hand moved in between my legs, entering into my pussy and rubbing my clit as he continued to press in and out, touching, teasing, fucking me harder and harder. There was a feeling of excitement and desire, a need that only grew more and more as time passed on. I didn't know what else to say, other than I was turned on, I was needy, horny, and I ached for him.

After a few more thrusts, he then pressed in, pushing his fingers upwards into me, touching my clit in the process. When he did that, I threw my back forward, tensing up, moaning out loud and in pleasure as he came inside of me.

The thrill of my orgasm hit me like a ton of bricks. It was so good, and the white that I saw in my eyes lasted a good moment or so. For a long time, I definitely didn't know what else I could do, or even what to say either. That's when he pulled back, looking at me with a smile on his face.

"There we go. Nice and punished," he said.

Sure, it may be a punishment to him, but I actually enjoyed this a whole lot more than I cared to let on. I mean, I wouldn't mind doing this again. But I didn't want to have it on punishing terms either.

"Yeah, I'm definitely learning my lesson," I told him.

"Good. As you should be. I don't want any more shit broken again. But...I did have a bit of fun with you. I'm surprised you took that so easily," he said.

In truth, I did have a fantasy about being taken and fucked in the ass like this. But I wouldn't dare tell him.

"Well I'm definitely quite happy with the results of this," I told him.

"Sure," he replied.

We looked at one another, his face still stern.

"But, I'm not letting you off the hook," he said.

"What do you mean?" I asked.

Was he really going to penalize me more for this.

"I never want to see you do this again. But, if you do accidentally do this, consider this to be the punishment. Perhaps a little bit harder," he said.

The sound of those last couple of words excited me. I mean, I wasn't trying to say that I wanted to be punished, but maybe I was as well.

"Yeah, I wouldn't mind that kind of punishment," I told him.

"I'm sure you wouldn't. and I can give you and even greater punishment too, if you're up for it," he said.

I'm sure this implied something else, and not necessarily actual punishments, so I nodded.

"Indeed. I'd like that," I said.

He gave me a smile, and then he walked on out. I laid there, satisfied by the treatment that this man gave to me, but I also wondered what else may happen next.

What did he have in store for me? Perhaps there was a lot that he wasn't just going to tell me. I quickly left the room, heading into the bathroom once more. Despite having an orgasm, I was turned on once again, pulling my dress up, teasing myself, thinking about the fact that his cum was still in my ass.

The idea of this thrilled me, turned me on, and made me excited for what would happen next. I don't know why, but there was something exciting and fun about all of this. I continued to push my fingers in and out, wondering how he'd feel inside my other holes, and I let out a small sigh, enjoying this.

I quickly relieved myself, but then, as I got out, I saw him there.

"By the way, I have one last punishment to give to you," he said.

Did he hear me? I don't even know, but I stopped, tensing up.

"What do you mean?" I inquired.

"This," he simply said.

He leaned in, capturing my lips with his own. We kissed passionately for a moment there before pulling away, smiling in contentment.

"I'm going to have a lot of fun with you throughout the next few months. Or however long you want to stay," he said.

"I am too," I replied.

Gregory gave me a small smirk, one that screamed he was enjoying this just as much as I was, and then, he quickly left the area, leaving me there. As I sat there trying to figure out what else to do, or even what to say, I took a moment to figure out just what was next.

I mean, I wouldn't mind more of whatever this is, but I also wondered what he'd do now. I wanted to ask, but also...I wanted to keep up the fun, the games, and the way he continued to turn me on like this.

I didn't know what he would have in store for me next but it did mean that I'd head on over to the bathroom, relieving myself every so often.

I left that night completely smitten, but also curious about what the next plans were. What did he have in store for me? What did he want now? I don't even know, but I could tell it was the beginning of something else.

There was a thrill that came with showing him my special skill. The one that I had that I sued my mouth with, the one that I could show off to others, including him. but I wanted to share it with him again. His cock was nice and thick, big and wonderful, and I already missed the taste of it on my mouth.

Maybe I'd get a chance to do this again sooner than later. I wasn't sure though, mostly because I didn't know what was next. But I did love this job, and I wasn't going to get rid of it if I could.

Teacher's Pet

"Alright, you have till the third to get this completed. Got it," I said to the class.

I taught biology at the local college, a fun little class for most of the students. But I didn't make it easy. That's the thrill of having a job like this. I could teach them while also making it challenging and fun.

And challenging I did. I made sure that the class wasn't too easy for most of the students either. As I gave them the assignment, my eyes locked with Marcus.

Marcus was a bit of an underachiever. He would do the work sure, but he always seemed to be behind. Was it on purpose? I didn't even know anymore, but there was also that feeling that he was doing this for some reason, to stand out, and it bothered me that he acted this way.

As the students left, Marcus and I locked eyes. I walked on over to his desk, holding my clipboard in my hands.

"Marcus," I said with a deadpanned tone.

"Hey there Hannah," he said.

"It's Miss Davidson," I said to him.

"Sorry," he said, flushing crimson.

"It's fine. Well, I found out that your grades are suffering once again. What's been going on? This isn't like you," I told him.

He pursed his lips, pausing and trying to think of an excuse. He didn't really have one, and it made me frustrated that this was even happening at this point.

"It's just....I'm sorry Miss Davidson, I'm just struggling," he told me.

"Well, why do you keep struggling? Do you...need some extra tutoring?" I asked.

The truth was, I wouldn't mind giving Marcus a little bit of extra tutoring. He was a young man, with long, sexy dark hair, big brown eyes, and looked adorable. I wasn't going to lie, I did find him cute, in a...corruptible sort of way.

He paused, flushing in response.

"It's nothing. I'm just...a bit embarrassed," he said.

"It's okay to be embarrassed," I told him.

"Well it's more like...I keep getting distracted. But maybe a little bit of tutoring could help me too," he said.

Distracted? By what though? I looked at him, unsure of what he meant by that, but the least that I could do was try to help him out.

"Sure, I think I can help you out," I told him.

"Alright," he said with a smile on his face.

And that's how the tutoring sessions began. Marcus was a smart student, but he always seemed to struggle in our sessions. Was there something else there? I didn't know for sure. I was struggling myself to understand what else to say here, other than of course, that I wanted to be the best teacher that I was to him.

We worked together over the next couple of weeks, trying to strive for the best that we could. But Marcus just...he just kept screwing around. It was getting on my nerves.

"Alright Marcus, what the hell is going on?" I asked him after one of the tutoring sessions. I felt like the little bastard was doing this shit on purpose, but I'm not even sure anymore.

"I don't know! I just...I can't seem to get it. I feel like a fucking moron," he said.

"You should know better than this Marcus. You can't seem to get this right though, so what the hell gives?" I asked him.

He paused, flushing as he looked at me with a nervous look. There was obviously something else there. He wanted to say something, but he didn't.

So what the hell was it.

"Come on, spit it out," I snapped at him.

He looked at me, nervous as all hell, and then finally, he spoke.

"It's you," he said to me.

"What about me? I'm your professor, and I'm trying to help you get to the top of the class," I told him.

He flushed, looking me in the eyes as he mentioned this.

"I'm sorry, it's a little bit embarrassing," he admitted.

"Well, you can either spit this out and we go about our evening, or you make this awkward for both of us. Or maybe...a little bit of motivation is what you're getting at?" I teased.

"No it's just! You're really pretty," he said to me.

Gosh this guy was fun. He was nineteen, fresh and young, and I mean...I wasn't the youngest woman out there, but I did have a bit of age, and some experience.

"Well Mark, perhaps we can make a little deal," I stated to him.

He looked at me with surprise on his face.

"What do you mean?" he asked me.

This was fun to do. I wondered if he would let me tease him.

"Tell you what, why don't you...help me out with a few things. I'm going to need you as a special helper for the next few classes, and I can make you my pet. If you satisfy me enough, I guess I can of course let you get away with a passing grade in this class," I told him with a devilish smile.

He looked at me, gulping in surprise, anticipation and the like.

"Wait, you mean like….like sexually?" he said.

"That's what you want, right? I mean, I can see your cock hardening there," I said to him. I raised my hell, lightly digging it into there. He let out a small cry, not of pain, but of arousal.

"What's that? You like my foot on your pathetic dick?" I said.

"Y-yes," he said.

He was submissive. This would be a whole lot of fun.

"Alright, we can keep this our little secret. On one condition: you better not dare tell anyone else," I told him.

If he did that, we'd both be fucked.

"Or else I'll fail, right?"

"That, and so much more. I can make your life hell, if you let out a peep. If you do this for me…we can have a little bit of fun," I offered.

I knew that there was a risk here, but there was something fun about taking this young man under my wing, making him my pet, and using him for a variety of things. After a bit of a pause, he took a deep breath, flushing.

"Yeah…I'd like that," he said to me.

"Good. I see that we're on the same page then. How sweet," I told him.

I liked that he was already agreeing to this. It made the next few things that I did a whole lot of fun.

That's when this little adventure began. I set up a small little contract. I was a dominatrix on the side, and I never let clients go off without those. But there was also the fact that I didn't want this little shit to let out a peep or anything either. After he signed it, that's when the real fun began, and when we both began to have the most fun relationship ever.

When he got in early that period, I smiled.

"Alright, get under the desk," I said.

"W-what do you mean?" he said.

"I'm going to use you as my pet. You're to…satisfy me while I conduct these exams. Don't worry, I'll give it to you later, and you can pass, but you're to take care of me. If you don't make me cum, you will be punished," I said to him.

He flushed, but then nodded. He went underneath the desk, and I got the handcuffs, cuffing him underneath the desk so that he didn't escape, and no other students saw. I sat down there, looking down at him as he looked at me with those big eyes.

Fuck he was cute. I loved teasing this man like this. He then moved his hands to my thighs, which caused me to jerk in surprise at his actions.

It was fun to tease him like this. With the nervousness that he had, the way his eyes continuously glazed over me, that little look of need that he had...this was more fun for me than I cared to admit.

I wanted him to be a good little pet for me.

He looked at me with expectant eyes as I sat down, motioning for the students to grab the papers. I then smiled.

"You have fifty minutes," I said to them coldly, looking around at all of them as they stared at me in the eyes.

They started to take the exam, and I felt the hands move a little bit higher. Shortly after, he gripped my milky, soft thighs, spreading them apart. He licked them, causing me to grip the desk a little bit, shivering with delight.

Such a good pet.

I looked over at the other students, who seemed to be furiously getting started with the papers. I grabbed a book, trying to get my mind off of this, when suddenly, I felt a tongue near my entrance.

I tensed up, struggling to keep it together. I moved my hands downwards, pulling my skirt upwards. I made sure not to wear panties this go. Suddenly, I felt the tongue move against my clit, licking it slightly as I shivered, trying to hold back a moan of pleasure.

"You okay there?" one of the students asked.

I shopped ,my head around, looking at one of the women who was in the class. She had short brown hair, big blue eyes, and a bit of an awkward gait.

"Yes, sorry. Do you have a question?" I asked her.

Suddenly, I felt his tongue move closer towards my entrance, teasing me there. I had to hold back. I wasn't going to sit there and just let him have this. The girl who was there furrowed her brows.

"Well, I was wondering with this one...what if there are two answers for this?" she said.

Fuck, it was a struggle just to form words at this point. I looked at her, a hesitant glance on my face.

"Then just....try to find the one that best fits the scenario," I explained to her, cupping my lips as I tried to hold back the obvious moan that almost escaped my mouth.

"Are you sure that you're okay?" she asked.

"Yes, I'm fine," I choked out.

This little bastard was already inside, using his tongue to tease and pleasure me. He was very skillful, moving it in and out, fucking me with that appendage. I was already feeling my composure slowly come apart, but I wasn't going to sit there and let the little bastard get the best of me.

"Anyways, just choose the ones that best fit, and from there, you can continue," I told her.

She nodded, and the other students continued this. By this point, I was so close. I pushed my thighs around his face, moving my hips a little bit, trying to make sure that not a soul saw the way my body moved. Until finally, after a few more moments, I tensed up, biting my lip, feeling the pleasure of my orgasm suddenly take me.

I let out a long sigh, and a couple of the students looked up at me, trying to figure out what was going on. But I gave them a small smile, enjoying the way that they seemed so confused. It was so lewd, it was definitely not what we were expecting to have today, but I couldn't get enough of this man, and there was clearly some fun to be had.

But I didn't know whether or not I could let this continue. My mind raced, my heart skipping a beat every now and then. He continued to service me, the sensitivity of my clit suddenly the focus of his lips. He sucked and teased there, and before I knew it, I pushed my hips up, my juices flowing out, drenching his face in my release.

I continued this for the rest of the class, looking around, wondering if a damn soul knew anything about this. For a long time, it was just silence, and then, when it was all over, I finally sighed, trying my best to keep my wits about me.

After a little bit, I stood up, pushing my skirt down as I did this.

"Okay class….test is over," I said to them.

They all turned in their test, getting dangerously close to where Marcus was. He stayed quiet, even though I moved my foot up, my heel right up against his cock. He let out a small whimper, and I pushed it into his face, forcing the him to gag on the hell.

"Quiet," I whispered at him. I didn't want anyone to know about this. The class all finished up, and then, when the final person was gone, I went to the door, locking it, taking a deep breath. I went over, taking the handcuffs off of Marcus, pulling him forward.

"There you go. Good boy," I said to him.

"T-thank you teacher," he said, the way his eyes looked at me was both of that of lust, and of course of mild anxiety.

I looked down at his cock, seeing how it throbbed there. I scoffed.

"You're hard already. How pathetic," I said.

I pushed my heel up, resting it on his balls. I put a bit of pressure on there, causing the man to wince slightly.

"What's the matter? You like me squishing your pathetic cock with my heels? You want me to hit them? To use all of my force in this heel to hit them?" I said to him.

He whimpered, moaning.

"Yes, please mistress," he said.

The way he became so quiet and easy to work with was fun. I then lightly kicked them, causing him to let out both a moan, and a cry of slight pain.

"Wow, you're really just taking this so damn easily. Look at you," I pointed out, rubbing his balls and watching his eyes fall to the back of his head.

This was quite fun.

I continued to tease him, but then, I moved back, spreading my legs apart.

"Lick them," I told him.

He whimpered, looking at me as he moved down to my feet. He licked and teased them, cleaning my heels after they'd been shoved in his mouth, and after I rested them on his cock.

It was fun watching him slowly come apart like this. There was a thrill of course, in letting him lose all semblance of control like this. Enjoying the pleasure and need that grew within me as I watched him let out the cutest little series of moans and cries.

I continued this, watching with delight as he continued to finish the cleaning. When he was done, I pulled back, sighing in contentment.

"Look at you. Such a mess. Well, there is one thing that I'd like to give to you as a sort of…punishment. But maybe you'll enjoy it. Perhaps I'll reward you when we're done here," I said to him.

"W-what is it?" he asked.

I fumbled in my drawers, remembering that this was here. I grabbed three things: a bottle of lube, a toy, and the strapon that I kept in here the last couple of days. I was waiting for the right moment to use this on him, and right now, with the way he looked, how turned on and needy he was, there was something exciting about doing this to him now more than ever.

"You're going to use that on me?" he asked.

"Damn right I am. But I won't do it right away., I think I'll prepare you just a little bit before I give you my cock," I told him.

Seeing him there, all innocent and looking at me with a look of pure, unadulterated desire, it was quiet fun.

I started to pull down his pants, tossing them off the moment I got them off his body. He whimpered, and I touched his butt, rubbing it there.

"You have a nice ass. Very fuckable," I told him.

I gave it a smack, and he let out a gasp, tensing up and sighing as he continued to thrust forward. The little bastard was into this.

I smirked, enjoying this, and then, shortly afterwards, I lubed up the toy. It was pretty sizable, but of course, not so much that he wouldn't be able to take it.

I looked at his hole. It was so innocent-looking and fun to tease. I inserted the first part of the toy in there, watching him tense up, groaning in pleasure, enjoying the feeling that I gave to him. I shoved the toy a bit further into him, watching him tense up, and I enjoyed the delicious sounds of pleasure that he gave to me. I slowly pushed the rest of it into him, watching his hole take this slightly.

Even though he probably wouldn't admit it, the bastard definitely took this better than he'd ever care to admit. I pushed it fully in, watching it slowly disappear into him before waiting a moment, slowly pumping this in and out, watching with delight as he let out a small cry of pleasure, arching his hips forward?.

"Look at you, you're doing so good," I told him. He really was, much better than I thought. I didn't want to hurt him of course, but I also wanted to give him the pleasure that he desired. It was fun, that's for sure, and there was something exciting about doing this to him, making him lose all semblance of control, enjoying the pleasure of everything that was going on.

Before I knew it, I could see him taking it so easily that I knew he was ready. I pulled the toy out, hearing the groan of pleasure that echoed from his lips, and then, I slowly put the strapon onto my body, watching his eyes grow wide with delight. I pushed my hands to his hips, holding them there as I steadied myself, pressing into there.

This was fun. I stayed on the desk, letting the edge of the strapon get into him. at first, he was nervous, holding tightly and letting out a small series of groans. But then, before I knew it, io slowly pushed in deeper and deeper, watching his eyes widen and his cock start to thrust up there.

"Look at you! You're doing so damn well," I told him.

"T-thank you," he cried out.

I smiled, pushing him fully so that I was inside of him. when I was finally all the way in, I stayed like this for a bit, hearing him shiver with delight, and let out a series of moans.

"Look at you, getting fucked by your teacher like the little bitch that you are," I said to him, smacking his ass.

"Yes, please fuck this bitch," he cried out.

It was a thrill. It was fun. It was amazing watching him slowly come apart as I began to move in and out of him. at first, I took this slowly because I didn't want to hurt him in any sense. But then, I started to press in deeper and deeper, watching him tense up, the moans of excitement and need growing within him.

"Look at you. Such a fucking tease," I told him.

"Ahh," he cried out, tensing up slightly, enjoying the feeling of this. I loved seeing him all turned on and a mess, and it was then when, after a few more thrusts, I took it to the next level, pressing in deeper and deeper, enjoying the way that he lost all semblance of control here. There was a thrill to be had in this case, the fun that he would get to enjoy, and the pleasure that I could give to him.

I reached down, jerking his cock as I continued to pound his ass, and he let out a small cry. I knew he was getting close, and it was then when, after a few more thrusts, I started to hear him tense up. I grabbed his hips, plunging into him, and within moments, he shivered, crying out loud in pleasure, holding onto the desk as he came all over it.

I pulled out, sitting down and looking at him.

"Look at you. Now go clean that up," I said.

He looked at the desk and then at me, moving forward and then cleaning up the remains of his seed there. He licked it up, looking at me with a flushed face, and I smiled, watching him there, seeing the needy look in his eyes, and the rapt delight that he had.

This was so much fun, and I loved having the little pet there.

But when I saw him again, his cock was hard as a rock still. My eyes widened in shock.

"Damn, you're still hard?" I asked him.

"Y-yes," he said.

Oh this was going to be fun. I moved in between his legs, undoing a couple of buttons on my shirt, pulling my breasts out.

"Well, we can fix that. I haven't finished yet," I told him.

I wanted to go again. I placed my large, soft breasts against his shaft, moving them up and down. I spat on them to lubricate, moving them slightly, and then, as I did that, he cried out.

"Fuck," he said to me, holding onto me as I did this. I smiled, moving against him. This was fun, and I loved seeing him like this, but I knew that I needed something more, something greater.

I then moved back slightly, smiling at him as I straddled his hips, looking into his eyes as he stared at me.

"What are you—"

"Don't worry, you're going to enjoy this," I said.

I pushed him onto the desk, giving him a smile as I slowly sank into him. I watched his eyes begin to widen as I pushed all the way down, sinking there and feeling him. He held onto me, shivering with delight as he cried out, my body suddenly tensing up as I looked at him. There was an excitement that was there. It was utterly intoxicating, making me want more and more. The anticipation of this was to die for, a delightful activity that would only make me ache for more, and make me want him too.

When I got all the way down, we looked at one another, a smile on my face as I slowly started to move up and down. He held onto me, his eyes wide with shock and pleasure.

"Holy...shit," he said to me.

"What's the matter? You enjoying this?" I said to him with a smirk, moving my hips and up and down.

He immediately groaned, holding onto me for dear life as I shook my body around, jerking my hips slightly, watching his eyes widen in surprise at the teasing that I did. This was getting kind of fun, that's for sure. With everything going on, I knew that he was enjoying this, and it gave me great delight to see him slowly losing his composure there.

For a long time, I moved my hips, feeling his cock hit me in all of the right spots. I looked down, seeing him there, completely turned on and enjoying everything that came out of this. I wasn't going to lie, he felt amazing too.

His hands moved up towards my breasts, touching them slightly, and I couldn't help but moan in response to all of this. I suddenly began to tense up as he began to press himself upwards. I angled my hips, and after a few more moments, I slowly started to feel my entire body give way, moving forward as I cried out, enjoying the sensation of this. I then came hard, feeling it all just completely decimate me, making me suddenly lose all control, the enjoyment of this driving me insane.

After a brief second, I watched him pull back, looking at me. The cum dripped out of me, and I felt like I was losing my mind. I struggled to catch my breath for a bit, but there was definitely a feeling of enticement as we looked at one another.

"You good?" I asked him.

"Yeah," he said.

I quickly got myself together, looking around. I checked outside the classroom to make sure that nobody ended up seeing us. I hoped to god that nobody did. But who knows, I sometimes didn't get lucky with this shit, that's for sure.

For a moment, neither of us said anything, both of us not sure of what to say next about any of this. I mean, I enjoyed the hell out of it, but I knew that it was definitely a taboo thing. We didn't want others to know about it.

"Wow," he said, getting his pants and shirt back on.

"Yeah, wow is right," I admitted.

I can't believe I did all of that. But I could tell that he didn't seem to mind a damn part of it. I looked over at Marcus, who was flushing crimson.

"Something the matter?" I asked him.

"Well it's just...wow," he said.

"Cat got your tongue?" I teased.

"Maybe it does. Or maybe...I just liked that a whole fuckload," he told me.

I chuckled, seeing the happiness on his face, the grin that he had.

"Well, I know that you did want me to show you what I've got, and I aim to please," I told him.

"You're right. And you do," he said.

I laughed, seeing the look of pure desire on his face. But there was that curiosity on what was next, on what he wanted next, and for a moment, we didn't say a word.

"So. I guess we should talk about what this means for both of us," I told him.

"Yeah. What does it mean?" he asked me.

"It depends. What do you want from this Marcus?" I asked him.

"I just want good grades. I don't care about much else," he said.

"So....if you want, we can continue this. I'll give you good grades if you continue to be my pet...." I offered to him. I knew that this was a bit of a different situation than what we both thought about, but I could tell that he was enjoying this.

"Are you...sure about that?" he asked.

"Course. I liked it, and I know that you did too," I replied with a smile.

And liked it was a bit of an understatement. He came twice, and there was obviously that need for more that came from this.

"Okay. well I like it. And maybe you can...teach me a few things too," he said.

"You mean like how to please a woman?" I said with a wink.

"Yeah. I'm a bit awkward, and well...I do like girls I'm just shit at talking to them. But I get along with you super well. It's strange," he said.

"Well, sometimes it's like that Marcus. But if you want....we can continue this if that's what you're into," I offered to him. I knew that this would be a risky game, and that one of us could get in big trouble at any point if it's found out.

But at the same time, I loved it. I loved the fact that he was enjoying this as much as I was, and that there was an obvious need for more that came from this too.

"Yeah, I'd like to play this...this risky game," he said.

"Good. I'd like that too," I replied.

We both nodded in agreement, a bit of a small thing that both of us knew that we wanted. There was clearly a lust that was there, a desire for more, a pleasure that we both could enjoy, and I knew that he'd like this too.

We both agreed to start seeing one another for sessions like this once a week, and perhaps more if we ended up deciding to take things like this. I had no clue what in the world would transpire next, or even how things would go. I just felt a bit of a lustful excitement that came out of this.

He was fun to tease and please, and I would be lying if I said I didn't enjoy this either. It's not every day I got to have fun with a young man like this. After we both sat down and agreed to it, we ended up leaving, and I checked the clients that I had later on that night.

There wasn't much, but it was quite fun to see that I could go from dominating one man to another man. I just liked doing this, making men feel good, and making them squirm under me.

Marcus and I agreed to continue this for as long as we wanted to. He texted me saying that he had a good time, but his butt hurt. I laughed, realizing that I did go a little bit harder on him than I meant to. I told him to go ice it, since that probably would be the best way to handle it. After the phone clicked off, I sat there, thinking about what may happen next.

What was the future of this? What would happen with my teaching career? I started to grade the papers, looking for Marcus's name. I left him a B, since he did a good job and did pass, but there was always room for improvement. I made up a fake little exam and his name. even though this was wrong, I didn't really care in a way. I was having my fun, and it's clear that he enjoyed this too.

Marcus was definitely the teacher's pet, and he was a pet that I would keep around for as long as I could, and to tease and play around with till he couldn't take any more of it.

Best friend's Secret

"Yay you made it," Charles said as I stepped in. I pulled off the hoodie that I had, revealing the black t-shirt that I wore.

"I told you I'd come," I told him.

"I know Roxy. I just really missed you," Charles said.

Charles and I had been best friends since I was very young, hell since he was very young. We were practically inseparable as kids, and so many people ended up telling us that we needed to be together. Although that didn't happen, there was always that bit of tension between the two of us, that innate desire for well...something more. And I'd be lying if I didn't think about that every so often.

But Charles was also my best friend, and he weas a renowned businessman. He apparently had a girlfriend too, but I haven't seen her.

"Where's Debbie at?" I asked him.

Charles face froze. He looked around, and then at me. Obviously, there was something wrong.

"It's nothing. Sorry," he said.

"Come on man, you can't just act like that and expect me not to ask," I admitted to him.

I was worried. Debit and him seemed like such a power couple, that it made me almost a bit jealous. He was doing so well, but obviously, something was amiss.

He patted the seat, rushing over and grabbing a couple of glasses of wine, uncorking them and then bringing them over, filling up the glasses.

"I'm sorry Roxy. It's complicated with Debbie," he said.

"Did you two break up?" I asked him.

"Yeah. Sorry, I wanted to tell you in person. Yeah, we're not together anymore. For kind of a really dumb reason," he said to me.

What could possibly be so stupid that they'd break up? I always thought that Charles was the type of guy who never had petty breakups. I was almost a little bit jealous of him. but then, he sighed, taking a sip from his wine.

"Want to know what happened?" he asked.

"Yeah, hit me with it."

He paused, trying to figure out what else to say, and then he sighed.

"It's stupid. But we ended up fighting over kinks. We got upset with one another, and then…Debbie just left," he explained.

"Shit dude, I'm sorry. Wait…kinks? Like things you like to do in the bedroom? That's kind of a dumb thing to fight over. I always thought you were kind of vanilla too," I admitted to him.

Charles was cute, but I did think he had the vanilla tone to him. but he shook his head.

"You've got it wrong Roxy. I actually have wanted to explore kink with someone. I brought it up to Debbie, and instead of being supportive, she well...shamed me for what I liked. We had a heated argument, and I ended up telling her that if she can't accept me for who I am, then we can't do this. And then she just...left. Like that," he explained to me.

My heart sank as I heard that. I mean, it seems so petty to break up over that. It's weird though, since he was my best friend and all, that he didn't tell me about this.

Maybe it was because he was embarrassed by it.

It was kind of cute watching him awkwardly try to talk about whatever it was that he was beating around the bush about. Until finally, I spoke.

"Well what are you thinking about int terms of kink?" I asked him.

I'm not going to lie, I've thought about it too. I just haven't found someone that I trust enough to engage in that with. Maybe...this is a sign somehow.

He paused, looking at me and taking a deep breath.

"BDSM mostly. And well...I want to try impact play too," he said.

"Impact play you say?" I said to him.

Charles was my best friend, and he was pretty cute. He was tall, muscular, had a cute head of brown hair, hazel eyes, and a little bit of stubble on his chin. I'd be lying if I said I didn't have a crush on him.

"Yeah I just...want to try this with someone, and of course....let them experience it. But I know that it's a lot to ask for, and I thought that she'd be okay with it. But I guess he just wanted to keep everything vanilla for the most part," he said.

I felt bad that it happened to Charles. I mean, I could see the nervousness in asking, that's for sure. That's when I took a deep breath.

"I'm willing to try if you are," I told him.

He looked at me, confusion on his face.

"Wait, you mean—"

"Yeah. BDSM. I want to try it. Because well...maybe we both can learn something. I always have. and we can stay friends afterwards. I figured this may be something that may work better because we're so close," I told him.

We still were close friends. Maybe he didn't tell me about Debbie because he was worried about what I'd say. But then, he took a deep breath.

"Are you...sure about that? I don't want to make you uncomfortable," he said.

"Nah, you won't do any of that. You're pretty chill, and I know that deep down, you mean well," I told him.

He looked at me, flushing crimson.

"Yeah. Say, there is something I've wanted to tell you for a long time Roxy. You're my best friend, and someone that I know I can trust on and...I really do appreciate that," he said.

I blushed.

"Yeah. Same here. We've been best friends through thick and thin together. It's only natural," I said.

My heart skipped a beat. Charles was so cool, so chill, and we got along great. But now that we were together like this...I started to feel something more. Something deeper. And that's when I felt it.

He moved closer, his lips right over the edge of my own. He then pressed them there, sharing a kiss with me. For a second, I was a little bit nervous, but then, I relaxed, realizing that he weas a pretty damn good kisser. We stayed like this for a bit, until he pulled away, and then, he spoke.

"Sorry. Maybe that was too forward," he said.

"No you're good. If you were moving too fast, I would've told you," I said.

And I meant it. Charles was pretty cool about that sort of thing.

"So you're willing to...to try it?" he asked.

I was thinking about that. I mean, it would be just as friends, and obviously, the two of us were pretty damn close, so if there was something bad about this, we'd be able to stop it in its tracks.

"Yeah, but I think we do need a safe word," I told him.

"How about "Watermelon'," he said.

That would work. It wasn't my favorite fruit, nor did I hate it.

"Yeah, that works," I said.

"Yeah, if you say that, we stop. And I promise that I will," he told me.

"I know that you will. But thanks," I told him.

"Yeah I uh...bought a few things, and I wanted to try them, but I was a little nervous. When I brought it up to her, she completely shamed me for this, and she told me never to bring this up again," he said.

"Damn, I didn't expect Debbie to be such a bitch," I told him.

"Yeah, I was wrong about her too. But, there's not much we can do," he said.

There was a little bit of disappointment in his voice, but I didn't care. I did feel that connection, that growing desire, that need of course, for something more.

We went over to the bedroom, which looked barren now that Debbie was gone.

"Damn she moved everything out too," I said.

"Yeah, it fucking sucks," he said.

"Well, I guess I can take off my clothes then," I said jokingly.

I pulled off my shirt and pants, revealing the black bra and panties that I wore. I shook my jet-black hair, looking at him with green eyes and a smile that showed contentment and trust.

"Don't worry, I'm not going to act the same as her," I told him. it was weird to insist something like this, but he smiled warmly.

"Thank you. I do appreciate that," he said.

"Not a problem. You know that I'm here for you dude," I told him.

I was there for him, even though I knew that it was awkward for the two of us. He then moved over, grabbing the cuffs and blindfold.

"This was the first thing that I wanted to try," he said.

"Okay," I said.

He moved to my face, putting the blindfold over my eyes. This was the legit stuff.

"What don't you like?" he asked me.

"Anything too painful that draws blood really. I wouldn't mind trying things though," I said to him.

"Alright," he said.

I felt the excitement from this as he then put cuffs on my hands. we decided not on a gag for the first go, mostly because we were a bit nervous about all of this. Then, when he was done, he cuffed me to the bed, making me gasp.

"You good?" he asked.

"Yeah. Really good," I said.

I'd be lying if I said I didn't think that this was hot as hell. I liked the idea of being tied up, of losing all control, of feeling the excitement from this. His hands moved towards me, touching my sides, trailing them downwards towards my hips. I moved them upwards, letting out a small breath of surprise as I felt them there.

"You have an amazing body Roxy," he said.

"Thanks," I whimpered, feeling his hands over my thighs. He then moved his lips to my neck, lightly peppering kisses there. The touch felt a lot stronger than I expected, and soon, I moved my hips upwards, tensing up, enjoying the feeling of his soft, sensual kisses against my body, teasing, making me relish in pleasure, and enjoying it.

I shivered as I felt the touches slowly descend down my body, caressing every single part of me. I could feel my toes curling as his tongue and lips teased me.

"There you go. Good girl," he said.

"Ahh," I said, feeling the tension, the need, and the desire grow.

His hands hovered right over my breasts, giving them small, sensual touches. There was a heated desire within me, and then, his hands moved towards the back of my bra, undoing the clasp and moving the garment off of my body. It was a strapless bra, so easy to take off. But then, I felt the little touches descend downwards, touching right up against the edge of my nipples, little kisses and licks there.

Maybe it was because of the blindfold, but it felt like all touches were increased by manifold. There was something thrilling about this, something that I enjoyed, and something that I wanted. He continued to tease, pleasuring my body, enjoying the sounds that I ended up bestowing to him. He looked me in the eyes, smiling.

"There you go. You like this, don't you?" he said.

"Y-yes," I breathed out. He turned me into something that I thought I'd never become. A woman desperate for the touch.

His hands continued to touch my body, moving right up against my nipples, his fingers brushing against there, pinching the tips of it, making me shiver and cry out with pleasure and lust. He continued the touches, watching me tense up, moaning in pleasure as he did this. Every single touch, every single motion, it was all driving me slowly but surely to the point of madness, making me feel turned on, excited by this, enjoying the feeling of it all, wanting more from this man as he continued to touch, teasing every corner of my body.

I wanted him to pull on them, to make me feel both pain and pleasure. That's when he stopped.

Can I try something else? Clamps?" he asked me.

I flushed, realizing what he meant by that. I quickly nodded.

"Yeah," I told him.

"Alright," he told me. He soon moved his body over to somewhere, and then, I felt something tug on my nipples, holding them there. The pinching made me shiver, crying out loud in pleasure and desire. It hurt a little bit, but I also loved this, and I ached for more from him. He continued to tease them slightly, until I felt something else clamp down on me.

It was for my clit. He held the clamp there, securing it, and I shivered, moaning slightly in surprise at the action that he did. He let out a chuckle as he tugged on them slowly.

I cried out, feeling both pain and pleasure from this. It did hurt sure, but there was something about this which made me feel aroused, which made me excited, and in a strange way, I wanted more. There was that hunger there, that need within, that desire that made me get turned on and enjoyed every single aspect of this. There was that excitement which only made me ache for more.

After a bit, he then tugged on them harder, and I let out a garbled sound, enjoying the sensation of this. For a long time, I felt like I was at the mercy of this man, enjoying everything about this, and I knew that he liked it too. He continued this for a little bit, teasing me, watching me become a puddle of goo and pleasure in front of him. it was then when he pulled them off, and then, he moved to get something. I heard the sound of something being lit, and that's when I wanted to squirm.

Candles. He knew I was into wax play and temperature play.

"You're sure you're okay with wax play?" he said.

"Yes master," I breathed out, turned on by the words that came out of my mouth.

He chuckled.

"Damn, already calling me master. How cute," he said.

I let out a small cry as he continued to move towards me, and I could sense the wax dripping there precariously. I braced myself for this, enjoying the sensation of it all. He then dripped it down, causing me to tense up and moan in pleasure. I could feel the desire roving through my body, making me shiver with delight, enjoying the feeling of this. He then dripped it over the edge of my breast, causing me to shiver with delight.

It was a little bit warm, but not as bad as I expected it to be. I knew the candles burned a little bit lower in temperature. Probably because they didn't want you to burn the skin. He then dripped it there too, the dots forming something along my chest. There was something so arousing about being left out of control like this, feeling him just drip this down there, turning me on, causing me to tense up and shiver in pleasure.

"Fuck," I said, feeling it right over the edge of my nipple. It didn't go there directly, but there was that feeling of pleasure and desire that caused me to lose control at this point, making me tense up, causing an aching feeling in my body as I started to feel him drop it there again and again.

It was such a turnon. There was so much that made me feel very nervous, but this just...it just felt so damn good. It was amazing to feel, and I definitely liked the feeling of this too.

He continued to drop this down, piece by piece, until the wax was gone. I could feel it hardening slightly, but it wasn't an uncomfortable sensation.

"I made a cute design. Hopefully it stays," he said to me.

"Yeah," I replied.

There was a long pause, and then, I turned to him.

"If you want to try...impact play, you're free to," I told him.

"You're sure?"

"Yes. I want this. And if it becomes too much, I'll let you know," I said.

I had the safe word, but I didn't want to resort to that. I wanted to know what it would be like to be at the mercy of this man, unable to move out of the handcuffs, and unable of course, to see anything.

He flipped me around onto my back, pulling my hips upwards so my bottom was up in the air. He rubbed the edges of this, touching them slightly.

"Look at you, already arching and ready," he said to me.

"Yes," I breathed, turned on by the feeling of this.

He smirked, touching the edges of my ass. I let out a small cry of pleasure as I felt his hands right then and there.

"Look at you, all ready and willing," he said.

"I-I am," I said.

He then moved his hands away, and I sat there waiting for him. There was a long pause, and I wondered if he left for a moment. But then he came back, and when I felt the slap of his hand against my backside, I let out a small, choked sound of pleasure as I felt him hit me hard there. I suddenly tensed up, enjoying the feeling of this as he pushed his hand there, smacking me hard.

"There you are. Good girl. Look at you, enjoying all of this. You're so turned on, so needy. There's just something so damn hot about that," he said to me.

"Ahh! Yes," I said out loud, feeling him touch that spot again, smacking it hard. I shivered with delight, enjoying the feeling of this, loving the way that he just took me and used me like this.

He continued to spank me, and he did so very hard. It surprised me at how hard he was with this, but I didn't care. I liked the feeling of this too, and there was a thrill that came around with this, that need, that desire, and that lust for more as he did this.

He continued to spank me hard, and after a few more moments, he stopped moving himself away. I squirmed, shivering with delight as I wondered what he had planned next for me. I didn't know what he would really bring to the table with the impact play, but then I felt something a bit blunter, but covering a wider area touch the tips of my thighs and ass.

"This is a paddle. I want to see you turn red," he said.

"Yes...I want that too," I said.

He then raised it, smacking my ass hard with it. The indentations of this felt so damn different, and I let out a small cry of surprise as I felt this. He then smacked me again and again, each touch making me scream out a garbled cry of pleasure, my eyes tearing up at the pleasure and pain of the moment. He then smacked me again and again, hitting all parts of my ass with the paddle, making me cry out with pleasure and delight as he continued to touch me, tease me, making me lose all semblance of control as he continued this.

He then moved back, and I shivered with delight. Then, before I knew it, he had something else against my ass. It was a riding crop this time.

This one was small, but it would hit harder than the other paddle. I could feel him massaging every part of me, making me shiver and feel turned on. I felt the crop touch the very top of my pussy, rubbing my clit. I leaned into the touch, breathing out and moaning. He paddled that lightly, but that touch alone was enough to make me feel stimulation, to make me enjoy this and adore everything about this.

"Fuck," I cried out, feeling him press against there, hitting against there harder and harder, loving the feeling of this, enjoying the touch and teasing of it all.

He then moved back to my ass, massaging the area, but then, he moved away. I let out a small cry of need, feeling my hips move slightly, and that's when I felt it.

The crop made direct contact with my ass, making me shiver with delight, crying out in pleasure, feeling the aching moan and scream from this. They then hit me again and again, little Marks being made on my body, causing me to suddenly tense up, moaning out loud and in pleasure. I could feel them smiling at me without even seeing it. He enjoyed seeing me become a mess like this, and I loved being his mess.

I felt happy that I could give him this kind of control,, and there was a feeling of satisfaction as he smacked me again and again, harder and harder. He was careful around the other parts of my body, but I could feel the bruises and welts begin to form, and I loved it.

"Fuck!" I cried out, feeling him hit me hard. This was amazing, and my pussy was soaking wet at the sensations that I felt. I never knew how good this was.

But then, as quickly as it happened, he stopped, grabbing the final time. I thought it was a flogger. As I felt it hit my back, I shivered, crying out loud, enjoying the feeling of this. He continued to hit me, smacking me again and again, making me shiver, tense up, crying out loud and enjoying everything about this. He then smacked me all over, hitting every part of me, and I loved it. It was so good, the combination of both pain and pleasure turning me on.

When I felt it against my backside, lightly grazing my clit, I let out a small cry, tensing up, and that's when it hit me.

I didn't know that you could orgasm from this, but here we were, and I sat there, completely turned on, a total mess, and then, he pulled back, smiling at my body as I laid there.

"You good?" he said to me.

"Yes master but…"

He then let out a small grunt, and I felt the heat in my body rise. I know that this was supposed to be just the two of us experimenting, but I wanted something more. There was that desire for this, even though I wasn't sure what he thought about this.

"What is it?" he asked me.

"Well…I know this might be asking much but…I want you. Inside me master," I told him. I didn't know that I could say this. Perhaps it was the desire for him that had been sitting there for a long time.

"You sure?"

"Yes," I breathed out, the sound of need and desire in my voice making me feel like I would lose it if I didn't have him in there soon.

"Alright," he finally said after a brief moment. He then moved towards the drawer. I assume to get a condom, which was fine. He then spread me apart, slipping himself into there, and to my surprise...he was much bigger than I expected.

We never had this kind of relationship until now, but when I felt his cock all the way inside of me, filling me up, I suddenly felt turned on, enjoying the feeling of all of this. I felt like...everything was slowly starting to grow blank. I loved the feeling of pleasure that he provided to me, but then, when he got even deeper, I suddenly lost it.

He pushed all the way in, filling me up, making me shiver with delight, suddenly shocked by the feeling of all of this. He then pressed in, then moving out, and he soon moved in and out of me, causing me to slowly but surely lose all semblance of control, enjoying the sensation of everything that was to come. He continued to thrust in hard, feeling me tense up underneath him, and I could feel his hands against my ass.

"Look at you, so turned on for me. You feel amazing too," he said.

"Yes," I said, feeling the rush in my body.

I knew I was close again, and judging from the thrusts and how fast he was going, he was quite close too. And I loved that about him. There was that aching desire, that need for him, and that growing urge for more from this man. It was then when, after a few more thrusts, he reached down between my legs, whispering in my ear.

"I'm about to cum," he said.

"Then cum for me master. Cum in me!" I cried out.

He pushed in, letting out a small groan as he pressed deep, holding me there as he spilled his seed, the warm liquid within me. I shivered, feeling the heat that was there as I stayed there, looking forward. It was all blank still, and I felt a whole wave of pleasure too as it overtook me, causing me to enjoy everything about this.

For a long time, he simply held onto me, and we stayed like this, but then, he pulled back, grabbing the blindfold off of me, and helping me with the handcuffs. When it was all off, I sat there, looking around, my eyes slowly adjusting to the light once again.

"Damn," I told him.

"You okay?" he asked me.

"Yeah. Amazing actually," I told him.

This was definitely the best that I've felt in a long time, and I wasn't going to lie about that one.

"You sure? I didn't want to hurt you or anything, did I?" he asked me.

"No I'm fine," I told him.

He looked at me with a smile on his face.

83

"Good. I didn't want to hurt you on accident," he said.

"Nah, you have to do more than that to hurt me," I said with a chuckle.

"Well, I don't want to hurt you on accident. But that was a lot of fun," he said.

"Yeah," I replied.

I got up, wincing slightly. I looked down, seeing the welts and bruises forming on my butt.

"We should probably get some cream on those," he said.

"Yeah," I replied.

He brought some antibiotic cream, rubbing it in. it stung slightly, but also I enjoyed the feeling of his hands there. He continued to touch me, rubbing it in fully.

"There we go," he said.

I pulled back, looking into his eyes with surprise.

"Thank you. But...did you enjoy doing it? I know that this was to explore your kink, but I wanted to make sure this was what you wanted too," I said to him.

He nodded.

"I really did. I had a wonderful time," he told me.

I smiled, feeling relieved by that.

"Same here. Honestly...if you want to do it again, I'd be all great with that," I told him. The truth was, I enjoyed him, and the feelings that I had for him were real.

"Are you…sure about that? I don't want to hurt you," he said to me.

"Nah, you're not hurting me. In fact, I enjoyed this," I told him.

He sighed, happiness on his face.

"Okay good. I was a bit worried, but I can see it in your eyes. You're an amazing woman Roxy, and well,, maybe I did have a crush on you," he told me.

"Yeah, I did too. Maybe we can see where this will end up," I told him.

"Maybe we can," he replied.

We looked at one another, seeing the sparkle in one another's eyes. It was weird, what I thought would just be a normal meeting between friends turned into something…much much more. When we kissed, I felt a shiver in my body, the sparkle that I saw in his eyes. There was that feeling of excitement and desire that only made me ache for him more and more. With every single look, every single touch, I felt like my whole body was ignited, a desire that only grew even more so as time went on.

"Yeah, I wouldn't mind that. Of course, as long as you're cool with this," he said to me.

"I'd love it," I told him.

We looked into one another's eyes, giving a kiss once again. It was long, passionate, and something that I thoroughly enjoyed. As we stayed there, making out with one another, it felt like we were both impassioned there. It was the moment I'd been waiting for.

We spent the rest of the night kissing, talking to one another about what we liked and didn't like, and everything in between. There was that feeling of desire, that excitement which only made me ache for more, and that need too. We stayed like this for a long time, and then, later on that night we stayed over.

"I didn't expect things to work out like this," Charles admitted. I didn't think that this would work either, but here we are.

"Well, sometimes the unexpected happens," I told him.

"You're damn right, and you're an unexpected surprise that I can't get enough," he admitted to me.

I smiled, feeling the excitement and growth between us start to become more obvious. There was that feeling that made me smile, that excitement that made me feel good. We stayed together, both of us enjoying one another, and the feeling of the future strong for both of us.

Charles told me his secret, and I'd be lying if I didn't feel the same way. He was really good wat what he did though, and there was definitely a heated desire for more as well. A part of me wondered what may happen next, or even what we may get into, but I guess that's another play session to look forward to, and something that we could enjoy down the road, together as we explored one another's bodies, and the secrets that we had.

Pleasing the Donors

This was it.

I clutched the papers, realizing that I'd be meeting with some of the biggest donors to my campaign. I knew that it could reflect great or terribly on me, I just wanted to hope for the best. I had the plan all set out in place.

If the donors agreed to this, it would put my product on the map. I had the plan, just needed the financial assistance, and coming to this exposition with everything in place excited me.

I showed a couple of them earlier when they walked by the booth. But this would be a roundtable of all five of the biggest investors in kitchen and baking products. And I hoped that I'd stand out.

This was my dream. To be supported by one of these guys, and to make it work. That's what made me excited about this. I could change my whole goddamn life around just by making a couple of small changes, and I hoped that they'd understand, and feel the same way. I took a deep breath, making sure I had everything in place.

"Okay Mindy, you can do this," I said to myself.

I wanted to make this work. I wanted nothing more than for this to just go swimmingly.? I then opened the door, looking at the round table.

Five of the biggest investors all in one place. What I didn't realize was they were all young and attractive. The one at the center was the top-ranking CEO of one of the biggest appliance manufacturers, a guy named AJ. To his right was a man named Adam, who was a bit intimidating, but he gave me a small smile as I walked on in. next to him was Landon, who was one of the newer investors, but had a sizable income from his own investments in a variety of different companies.

To the right of AJ sat George, who was one of the older ones, but still he was barely over 40, and he looked like he was still in his 20s. his silvery-gray hair looked nice, and I couldn't help but feel my lips salivate at the sight of him.

Then finally, there was Craig. Craig was a bit controversial with long, black hair with blue streaks in it, a couple of piercings, and he tended to wear something different from the normal attire of business suits that these five usually had. They all looked at me as I gave them all a weak smile, feeling my heart skip a beat.

Don't fuck this one up Mindy.

"Hey there. I'm here to show off my product. I think it was craig and Adam who saw it on the showroom floor, but I wanted to show everyone," I explained to them.

"Yes, I'd love to see it," AJ said with a smile.

"Yes, me too," George said with a nod.

Landon also nodded. Adam and Craig both sat there, looking at me with a curious glance as I tried to get myself together.

To say I was nervous was a goddamn understatement. I didn't want to fuck this one up. Not now. Not after all that I've worked towards. But I took a deep breath, steeling myself as I got together for what would happen next.

:Alright so first of all this is the bake chop. It's a way to chop up cakes and other slices into pieces while it is baking. That way, it saves the time of cutting it up. It's a precise instrument, and it can do up to 16 servings! You just need to tell it what to do and all," I said, feeling my lips grow dry at the way they looked at me.

None of them showed any obvious emotions yet, which made me nervous. I had no fucking clue what would happen. I mean, they were all attractive men, and me, just some brown-haired mousey inventor, felt like I was out of my league with everyone there. But I had to keep my shit together. R that was the only thing that I knew how to do effectively, and easily.

But I didn't know what else would happen to me next. I wanted things to be different, to go well, but I had no clue what would happen next to me.

"So show me," George said.

"Yeah I'd love to see a demonstration," AJ said.

"Right uh...here's a cake. Let's put it in," I said.

I got the cake out, feeling all of their eyes on me. I put it in the machine, and then placed it in the oven. A few minutes later I pressed the button, and then, it cut up the cakes. I pulled it out, giving it to them.

"As you can see, the product does work. This also ties into the smart spatula I have. it will help determine the temperature of some of the items that you have in order to give the most perfect result. That way you're not overcooking any of your foods and know when to turn it," I explained to them.

"very interesting," Adam said, nodding in response.

"Yes, quite the inventions you've got there Mindy," AJ said.

"Thanks, I try," I replied with a smile.

I showed off both of these, and they all looked at me with interest in their eyes.

This may be it. This may be the moment I'd been looking for.

"So yeah, that's my product. As you can see, it's the product of a lot of hours and work, and I'm trying my best to make sure it's right for everyone and all," I said.

"I see. Impressive. I think we've made our decision though," I heard AJ say to me.

I paused, surprised that they made such a decision right away. I thought they'd listen to other people, and then determine whether they would put their funding into one or another.

"What do you mean? I thought you guys had a lot of people to go through," I asked them.

"Well while we liked it, we didn't think this was suffice to win us over. We're sorry, but we can't accept this," AJ said.

George, Adam, Landon, and Craig all didn't say a damn thing. I looked at them with shock in my eyes, and abject fear at what may happen now.

Could this really be the end? I didn't want it to be. I wanted things to work itself out, but I felt like I just blew the one chance I had for things to go swimmingly.

So I sat there, trying to figure out what to tell them. But I had nothing. There was nothing left for me to say.

I was at a loss.

"Are you sure you won't listen?" I asked.

"You heard AJ. I'm sorry hun, but we don't see a financial opportunity in this one," he said with a bit of an annoyed tone, like he didn't want me here period.

I felt ashamed, unsure of what to say to them, and in truth, I wanted to just cry.

But I kept my face a bit stoic. That's the only thing that you could do in times like this.

I needed to think of something, anything that could work for me. and that's when I thought about it.

It was a stretch, but they were all guys. So maybe I could possibly use this to my advantage.

I started loosening my shirt, pulling the tie and the top button that I had off, exposing the ample cleavage that I had. That was one of the plus points that I had. I had nice cleavage, and good boobs, and I think that...there was a chance that this could work to my advantage.

At least that's what I wanted to hope.

I started to move my hips slightly, a smile on my face as I looked at them.

"Well perhaps we could...make an arrangement," I said.

I noticed AJ's eyes look downwards at me.

"You're serious," he said.

"Damn well I am," I said.

He looked me over, trying to figure out what he wanted to do. Would he fall for this, hook line and sinker? Or was I biting off more than I could chew.

Finally, he sighed.

"Well, let's take a vote. If the guys want to do this, then I suppose we can arrange something. If not, you'll leave and never come back," he snapped.

He was serious. I looked at him, nodding.

"Alright. Take your vote," I told them.

They started to raise their hands, each of them except for George agreeing to this. I didn't expect it to be this easy, but here I was, watching the fate of my business start to fall forward in the hands of all of these men.

"You guys are serious...right?" I asked him.

"We're making an exception for you. Don't think we'll agree to just anything," he said to me.

I knew they wouldn't just agree to anything. They were obviously going to need me to pay the fuck up, and I hated that I was putting my fate in this.

But also...I knew that this would be the beginning of the future for me, and if I could get their agreement on this...then everything would work out.

And I wanted things to work itself out.

I then moved myself so that I was on the desk, pulling the buttons of my shirt downwards.

"Then you can have me. in exchange, you fund all of the research and the products that I have," I said.

AJ looked me over, nodding.

"Very well. You heard her guys. This one is putting all of her fate in all of us," he said with a smile.

AJ looked at me, and I could sense that he had some big ass plans for me. was this really the smartest decision? I didn't even know anymore or even what I should say. I started to watch him move his hands downwards,

94

grabbing the buttons on my shirt, pulling them off with a forceful hand.

[I heard the rip of one of them, and I mentally hoped that it was one of the less obvious buttons, but the shirt was practically thrown off my body. A pair of hands moved towards my breasts, touching them there.

I looked up, seeing that it was Landon. He looked at my breasts, and then at me.

"I'm sorry but...I haven't gotten off in a long time and you look too good to resist," he said.

I smiled.

"Well I'm offering this. You remember our little deal," I told them.

They guys all started to let their hands wander against my body. A couple moved towards my breasts, a couple moved towards my pussy, cupping the heat there, and another moved towards my ass, grabbing it. I didn't expect this much attention.

The one who seemed to be the least into this was George, but a part of me wondered if he was just playing the part. Maybe he liked this a lot, and he didn't want to deal with any of this shit.

But then I felt AJ move himself so that he was right over my body, my hands splayed out. He looked into my eyes, a look of pure, raw need on his face.

"There we are," he told me.

"Yeah," I said.

He moved his hands towards my breasts, touching the very tips of thumb, cupping the edges of my breasts. He teased them from outside of the contents of my bra, the large mounds shaking slightly like jello. I flushed, moaning slightly at the way that this felt, at the pleasure that I was feeling.

I then felt another pair of hands move towards the back of my bra. It had to be George. He undid it with finesse, letting the garment tumble down, revealing my large, aching mounds. I flushed, looking at him as he grabbed the orbs, touching them there.

"Look at you," he said, smiling at me. He teased the tips of my nipples while lightly licking my neck. I let out a small moan, feeling my body react almost immediately to the sensation of this. That isn't to say that I was going to make a fuss. His hands were a bit rougher, and I winced slightly as I looked over at the other guys.

I then noticed AJ move towards the tip of my other nipple, pressing there with his fingers, rubbing it slowly, surely, and enough to make me shiver and cry out, enjoying the sensation of this. I knew that he was enjoying the sounds I made, and my body grew hot from the touch of his hands alone.

It felt good, and I could feel my entire body melting to the pleasure of the flesh, the excitement and need that this brought to me.

There was that need for more, that craving for more, and that desire to just…lose all semblance of control and give it all up.

I began to feel his lips suck on one of my nipples. Then, I felt Landon move to the other one, lightly peppering kisses there, touching the very edge of it with his lips before letting his tongue snake out, touching, teasing, playing with that there. I felt the heat rise through my body, starting to flood on through, causing a feeling of desire to envelope through every fiber of my being, making me enjoy the feeling of this too.

They continued to tease me, while I felt a hand down there, cupping the heat of my body. I shivered, moaning out loud as I felt that area get rubbed and rubbed once again. I felt everything just slowly melt, the pleasure and excitement of the moment driving me slowly to the precipice of madness. I wanted more, I craved more, and I knew that, no matter what happened next, they'd all make me feel good.

I believe it was Adam's hand that was against there, teasing me while the other hands were all over, teasing every part of my body. Craig moved towards my neck, licking and nibbling on the flesh there, causing me to let out a small breathing sigh of relief, the pleasure of the moment, the excitement of what was going on, all of this making me feel desire that I wasn't expecting to enjoy and feel either.

I loved this, and I knew that they all wouldn't get enough. Adam continued to rub me, touching the outside while his tongue moved towards the tip of my clit, rubbing against there making me shiver with delight and man out loud, and with a roaming pleasure that I only could fathom that would exist.

They continued this for a long time, until I felt AJ pull back, looking at all of them, and then at me, a devilish smile on his face.

"Enough with this foreplay bullshit. I need to fuck you," he said.

The way he said those words made me shiver with delight. I wanted him to fuck me too. There was a riveting feeling that started to flow through me as I heard those words. He soon moved his hands downwards, undoing the skirt that I had, practically forcing it off of my body. I felt a bit on edge as his hands got slowly closer and closer to the edge of my pussy. I could feel the heat there, making me suddenly tense up, enjoying the sensation of this, and the need that grew with me.

I could feel his hands against my entrance, two fingers inside, and I suddenly felt my whole body tense up, the ache, the need the excitement and desire making me shiver with delight, start to drool and feel my hips buck.

His fingers slowly made their way inside, slightly teasing the very edges of this, making me shiver and moan, the need for more growing in me. His fingers were soft surprisingly, and when I felt them move upwards in that "Come hither" motion, I suddenly felt like I was losing all semblance of control, the need and desire only becoming more and more obvious with time.

His touches were enough to drive me crazy, and they were already making me shiver and melt as I could feel him touching every perfect place. I knew he enjoyed this as much as I did, and I soon noticed his hands move a bit upwards, also touching the tip of my clit too, rubbing there.

Even though this man was a hardy businessman he knew how to please a woman. just the touch of this alone was enough to make me feel all parts of myself start to stutter, and my whole body crave the touch of this man even more.

While he did that though, I felt something against the tip of my mouth. I looked over, and it was craig's cock. It was big, throbbing, and it looked ready for me. I opened my mouth willingly, feeling his cock slide down my throat.

"Shit your mouth feels good," he said.

I felt two cocks fall into each of my hands. upon further inspection it was Landon and Adam, who seemed adamant for something, whatever it might be. My body reacted with excitement to the idea of being able to service all of these cocks. Even though this was not what I normally did, I enjoyed being taken like this, enjoying the pleasures of the moment, and the excitement of the feelings that I felt as time started to go on.

I felt them all tease me, take me, pleasure me. I didn't have any way to really do much besides service all of these cocks. AJ continued to pump, before he spread me apart. He let out a small little grunt of excitement.

"God you look so good. I think it's time for the main event," he said.

I let out a small groan, feeling the heavy excitement of everything hit me like this. I noticed he was undoing his pants, pulling them off along with the belt to reveal the obvious erection in his pants. I looked at his cock for a brief moment before craig pushed his cock further down my throat, and I soon let out a small grunt of excitement.

I wanted this, and I knew that he wanted them too.

He quickly pushed himself in, and I let out a small scream as he filled me up. He was a lot bigger than I imagined, and I knew that I couldn't really say much with the cocks in my mouth and hands, but before I knew it, I felt him start to thrust a little bit faster.

A cock moved underneath my armpit, and I looked over, seeing that it was George who had it there. I didn't expect this, but the sliding sensation made him groan, and while I did focus on it for a bit, suddenly, I started to lose control, the excitement the pleasure and the feeling of it all was driving me crazy.

I knew that I couldn't get enough of this. They were all making me feel amazing, and there was clearly an excitement and need that came from all of this, which made me feel that desire for more.

AJ pulled my legs, spreading me apart, thrusting into me faster and harder. I loved the way it felt. He seemed to know exactly where to pleasure me. his thrusts were hitting all of the right areas, and I felt that hunger, that need, that desire for so much more start to hit me. he soon pushed all the way in, letting out a grunt.

That's when I felt it. His white seed enter into me, filling me up. He pulled out, the trail of cum start to escape my pussy.

"There we go. That was pretty good. Well boys, you can have the rest," he said.

That was surprising. I didn't expect AJ to just nut and go. But then I felt a pair of hands start to moved me, spinning me around so that I was on my hands and knees. Craig still had his cock in my mouth, and I wasn't going to give that up anytime soon, but then he pressed it in deeper, groaning.

"Holy fuck," he said, looking into my eyes. I felt the cock fall all the way down my throat, his balls right up against the edge of my lips. But I took it all readily, enjoying the pleasure the feelings that came out of this, and everything in between.

As he did this, I looked over at Landon, who was a bit nervous about this.

"There we go," Craig said. He looked up at Landon and then down at me.

"You know you can fuck her you know," he said.

Landon quickly nodded, moving so that his cock was right at my entrance. He slid himself all the way in, filling me up completely, and suddenly, I let out a low, guttural scream. I loved the way that this felt, the pleasure that came out of this, the excitement of the moment, it was all just…so perfect and I couldn't get enough of this. He continued to thrust in deep, enjoying the little whimpers and sounds that came out of this. Landon grabbed my hips, thrusting in deeper and deeper, making me cry out slightly.

"Look at her, she's taking all of this like a champ," Landon said.

"Yeah. She's great at sucking cock too," I heard Craig say.

I let out a series of small grunts, and then I looked up, seeing George there, his cock out, jerking it tot sight of my naked body as it got pleasured by both of them.

"God you're so hot. I'm sure that AJ was making the right decision with you," he said with a grunt.

I shivered, realizing that AJ was the one in charge of this. But I liked it, and I knew that they did too.

Landon pressed himself in, arching his hips and pressing upwards. I started to let out a small cry, enjoying the feeling of this, and I soon began to hold onto the desk, letting out cries as Craig fucked my mouth raw.

After a couple of moments, he tensed up, and I felt a little bit of his cum spray into my mouth. But then he pulled outwards, jerking off and letting the cum spit into my face.

I let out a small cough, but then I cried out as Landon held me, thrusting upwards hard, cumming deep inside of me. it felt amazing, and with the little hand against my clit, rubbing it, I lost all control.

I cried out, enjoying the feeling of this, my own orgasm overtaking me. it was all so damn perfect, so amazing, and I knew that there was only so much I could do at this point.

He finished up, pulling away, and I soon sighed. I enjoyed the feeling, but there was that sensation, that desire for more. And as I looked over at Adam and George, who were the last two, I felt an excitement and need grow within me.

"please. More," I told them.

I soon felt Adam flip me over, spreading me apart. I expected him to push himself into my pussy, but a finger moved downwards, teasing the edge of my pucker making me shiver with delight, and I cried out, enjoying the feeling of this.

"Holy...shit," I told him.

"You like that?" he asked.

"Yes. It's amazing," I told him.

He let out a chuckle as he started to tease the tip of my pucker, pressing two fingers inside that hole. I let out a chocked sound, enjoying the feeling of this. He added a few more fingers, till he had four inside of me, and I felt like I was losing control.

I needed him. I wanted him, and I knew that he was enjoying this as much as I was. He quickly pulled me into his arms, and I soon slid down, feeling his thighs against my backside. I felt his cock breach my ass. Even though it was a bit of a discomforted sensation and I was a little weirded out at first, as he got all the way to the very base, I suddenly let out a small cry, enjoying the feeling of this, and his cock filled me up completely.

He soon moved all the way in, making me cry out slightly. He soon let me move, feeling my hips as I bobbed up and down, moaning slightly.

But there was still George, who was jerking it to the sight. I thought he'd stay like that, but then, he grabbed my legs, spreading them apart as he slid inside of me.

I let out a cry, moaning in pleasure as I felt them both move in and out of me. Sometimes it would be at the same time, and that feeling of fullness was enough to drive me mad. Other times they'd alternate but I didn't care. Either way , I enjoyed the feelings that they provided to me, the pleasure that I got, and the way that their bodies just made me lose all semblance of control.

It was making me lose my mind, and I couldn't help but feel like I was so close to the edge.

George reached down, rubbing me, and then I felt that there was something hitting that one spot, that one part of me, and then, moments later, I tensed up, feeling like I was losing all semblance of control. I came hard, feeling my body tense up, enjoying the feeling of this.

Shortly afterwards, Adam pushed in, grunting as he filled me up completely.

Then there was George.

He pushed me onto the desk. I thought he'd just fuck me there, but instead he started to jerk off all over my body, making me shiver. When he came, dribbles of cum started to decorate my body, encasing my breasts, stomach, and other areas in white.

I felt like I was totally used by all of these guys, but I didn't care. This was exactly what I'd been waiting for. When they finished, I stayed there, taking a moment to bask in my orgasm.

I didn't mind this in the least, even though I'd been used by all of these men. There was something thrilling about this, something that made me ache for more, and something that I enjoyed.

"There we go," AJ said.

"Looks like she did well," Adam said.

"Yeah, that was really nice," Landon added.

"Indeed. We found a pretty good one," I heard Craig say.

"Yeah, even for how much of a desperate slut she was, she definitely was promising," I heard George finally add.

I didn't know whether or not this was the right thing to do, or if I had just completely fucked over myself and everything in between.

"So what did you guys think?" I finally said.

"Well, you certainly brought a lot to the table, and as some of the top supporters of many companies...I suppose we can give a little bit of support to you," AJ said with a wink.

I beamed. All of that work, and the hard work I did beforehand, paid off.

"Thank you. I promise that I won't let you down," I said.

"Course you won't. you certainly delivered on your promise too," AJ added.

"Yeah, I didn't expect you to go through with all of that. But here we are. I suppose we can let you have this one," Adam said. He was hesitant, but I think that was also just him playing hard to get.

"Yeah, we're pretty impressed with all that you did. Perhaps you do have some potential to add to the table," Craig added.

All of them seemed pretty happy, and there was clearly an exciting feeling that ghosted through my body. I started to smile.

"Great. I'm excited to continue this working relationship with you. Let me get cleaned up, and then I can do the paperwork," I said.

"Sure, take your time," AJ said.

I quickly made my way to the bathroom beforehand, and I cleaned up everything that was there. I was disgusted by the way I felt, but at the same time, I didn't regret what I did. Most people wouldn't dare do this, but honestly...I'm different from the rest.

In fact, this was definitely something that I enjoyed and I'd do it again.

I got myself together, and I prepared for coming back to see what they'd do next. When I got there, I stepped inside, the paperwork already nestled on the table, waiting for me to wrap up.

As I wrote down my name, I started to realize that this was the beginning of one hell of a relationship. It wasn't every day that I did this kind of shit, and honestly, most normal people wouldn't do this.

But I wasn't normal. I was someone who would stop at nothing to get what I wanted to get the recognition that was in place, and I knew for a fact that they were enjoying all of this too. I finished with the last of the paperwork, and AJ extended his hand.

"Well Mindy, you do drive a hard bargain, if I do say so myself," he said to me.

"Yeah, I sure as shit do," I told him.

"I take it that you find our little arrangement...fine then?" he asked.

"Yeah, for the most part I'm cool with it," I said.

In truth, I didn't know what this would mean for me, or even what would happen now, but I was just glad that I got to have something like this, and I was ready to see what would happen next.

When I left, I knew that it would be our little secret. The corporate donations would help my inventions get off the ground. While it wasn't considered the right thing to do in some cases, at the same time, I didn't care.

The future was brighter and I was way happier.

The Forbidden Patient

"Dr. Nadine, we need you in room 205," the voice on the intercom said.

"Alright," I muttered to myself.

Working at the regional psychiatric hospital as one of the top-leading psychiatrists was definitely not what I thought it'd be. In fact, it was much harder than I expected.
I was one of the top-ranking doctors that was in the area. In fact, I made sure that everyone was taken care of, and I made sure all medications and the like were intact. But I was also a normal doctor, who was in charge of medications for a variety of patients.

While most of the people I did see were typical psychiatric cases, in a few instances, there were those who were a little bit different.

And the patient in room 205 was different.

When I stepped inside, I immediately was met with what seemed to be the most attractive man I've ever seen. And also one of the most untouchable men as well.

William Merkins. The famous model. The guy with the body of Adonis, and a pearly-white smile that would make women swoon.

And he of course was the man I'd be seeing today. I just never expected him of all people here.

"William," I said to myself.

"You know me too? the other doctors kept asking for an autograph," he said to me.

"I see," I told him.

"Well, I'm here so I guess the secret is out," he said to me.

"What do you mean?"

"That I'm a fucking lunatic. My ex she...she called the cops on me. She thought that I was going to off myself or some stupid shit. They came, and then they brought me here. Said it'd be good for me. well I also was about to relapse. You know I've been to rehab, right?" he said.

I sure as fuck did, but because the latest tabloids would report on this shit.

"I do. But that's not why you're here, is it?" I asked him.

"No...I'm here because I want to live a normal fucking life. I'm so sick of feeling this way," he said to me.

"What do you mean?" I asked him.

He looked at me, sighing.

"It's complicated. I kind of came here because I needed a solution. And well...I didn't know where to look. I tried to ask others, but they kind of all blew me the fuck off. So I got a bit desperate. I should've been better about

110

my ex's feelings, but it also was a struggle. Have you ever had people just not listen to you? Like at all? And you want to scream for help but not a goddamn soul hears you?" he asked me.

I could get what he was getting at. I mean, I was a doctor after all.

"Yeah, I get that. You want to be heard. Is there anything personal you'd like to discuss?" I asked him.

He looked at me, flushing.

"Well mostly just about life. I came here for answers. And I heard you're one of the best around. I was worried you'd prescribe me meds and then go on your way and then—"

"No way," I snapped.

I looked at him, and then he nodded.

"Thanks, that's relieving. Well, I guess it's a crisis. I don't know whether I want to keep the modeling schtick up," he said.

"Well, anything in particular make you change your decision?" I asked him.

He started to nod.

"Yeah, lots of things. Just the modeling world is exhausting, and I don't know how much more of this shit I can take. I just need some advice, and I know that you've got the advice I'm looking for. And I'd...I'd like to talk about that. If that's okay," he said.

111

I nodded.

"Anything I can do to help. If you'd like, we can do therapy sessions and such too," I said.

I was a trained counselor, and that alone made him nod.

"Yeah, I'd appreciate that," he said to me.

We began to talk about this and that, and while I was doing my job, I couldn't help but flush a little bit when I saw his large, expansive body, the pecs he had, the washboard abs he possessed. It all made me want to lick my lips. I felt like I was slowly losing it, but I needed to keep it together.

For the patient's sake.

As we talked though, I could see the heat in his eyes, the look of desire. And I wondered if it was just me who was feeling this, or perhaps it was something more. Something deeper.

This went on for a little while. For the first week of counseling, we ended up talking about everything and anything. I discovered that he was having a goddamn crisis. It surprised me that he would be like this, but I guess that's the way life fizzled out at times, and honestly, I didn't blame him for feeling this way.

Shit was hard, and it was the least I could do to help the guy out.

I noticed that William was also not staring directly into my eyes when we talked, as if there was something bigger there. I wondered about that, but I didn't want to ask him about it. I felt that was wrong, like I was making a huge mistake if I did bother him about this.

Still...there was something about this which felt off.

I did notice his mood changed though during out sessions. At first, he was a bit stubborn, adamantly against talking about the pain from his past. But I'd reach out, touching his hand, looking him in the eyes.

"Trust me. I know it's scary now, but we'll make it. Together, " I told him.

"I know. Thank you for that doctor," he said.

And that's when things began to change. There was a connection there, something much bigger than a mere patient-doctor relationship. And I realized I was making a mistake too.

Then, it happened. One night during therapy.

"So tell me...has this caused you to develop any sorts of tendencies?" I asked him, writing down in my notes about his previous grappling with abusive women.

William sat there, listening to my words, and then...he nodded.

"Yeah, but it's an embarrassing revelation," he said.

"This is a doctor-patient confidentiality. Remember you can tell me anything," I told him.

Even though he was a famous celebrity, I could sense he was nervous about all that he had to say. I don't really blame him though. I mean, opening up about this is a struggle.

But then, he sighed.

"It's embarrassing," he added.

"Well if you don't talk about it now, you'll never heal you know," I said.

"You're right but...it doesn't make this any easier for me," he said.

"I'm not going to judge you, you know. We can keep this between us. Obviously I won't tell anyone about what's said during therapy and such," I explained.

I'd get in deep shit if I did that. After all, this is confidential, and it's supposed to be.

He took a moment to process what to say, taking a deep breath as he spoke.

"Fine. I guess I can tell you. But you promise to keep this a secret, right?" he asked me.

"Yeah, course. It's a secret," I said to him.

He looked around, and then back at me, sighing.

"Truth is...the abuse made me realize that I like a controlling woman. I want a woman to dominate me, but not hurt me. it wouldn't be abusive per se, but it's hard for me to take charge. I love it when women do," he said.

I flushed. I always liked taking charge over men. But I never told anyone about it. I wrote down the notes, pushing my hands through my red hair, looking at him.

"I'm sorry that you've struggled with a lot. but I get that. You want someone powerful," I told him.

"Yeah Nadine. And the thing is...I have always craved for a woman to just dominate me. To make me their bitch, and I know it's degenerate, but I can't stop thinking about it," he said.

"I see. As someone who is a bit more dominant-leaning, I get that. It's something you desire," I told him.

He then blushed, looking around, and then at me.

"That's I guess...why I wanted to ask you this. I know it's wrong, and I know that if I tell you, I'll probably be in deep shit. But I can't stop thinking about it. Ever since we started meeting for these kinds of sessions, I've felt the urge to tell you, but I have no idea what you'll think of it," he said.

"Whatever do you mean?" I asked.

He then blushed, looking away, and then turning to me.

"Could you...dominate me Nadine? It wouldn't just be for you, but it'd be for me too. I want to feel a woman overtake me, make me feel like I'm powerless. It's something I've desired more than I thought I ever wanted something, and I know that it's wrong, it's embarrassing, but I can't get my mind off of this," he said.

I couldn't believe I was hearing what he wanted. He wanted me to break this contract, to do...that.

And yet, I wanted to.

There was an urge there, something which continued to haunt me as he offered this.

"You're serious," I said.

"Yeah. I want you to do this. I promise that...we'll make it a secretive thing. I just want to be dominated by someone strong and powerful. Please. I feel this would help me immensely," he said to me.

I looked him in the eyes, and then I nodded.

"You promise confidentiality, correct?"

"Right. If anyone found out about this...you wouldn't be in trouble. I would be," he said.

"I could get my license taken away William," I told him.

"I know but....I also want to explore this. Just the two of us. It doesn't have to be a long-term thing. It can be just the two of us learning about one another. That's all," he said.

I pondered this. It was super risky, and the rational side of myself knew this. But that other side, the one that was curious about what may happen next, who wanted to explore this further, immediately smiled.

"Well, I guess we can settle this. Tell you what, get on the little lounge there and we can get started," I said.

He looked at me with a look of relief, and slight worry, but I simply smiled. I knew this would be new for both of us, but the truth was, I wanted to explore this too. I knew that it was wrong, that I'd get in serious trouble if a soul found this one out.

But I didn't care. I was horny and he seemed just as needy for me as I was him.

We'd also keep this a secret too. After all, he worked in the public, so if his image was fucked, we'd both be fucked.

Even though I knew for a fact that it was wrong, that I'd get in trouble, I had my case here for these types of moments for the off chance that I'd get to explore this further, that I'd get to enjoy this too.

I watched him as he sat there, looking me in the eyes, and I could see that anticipation that was there. Then, before I knew it, I started to grab the container, bringing it in here.

The truth was, I was a dominatrix on the side. It was mostly when I was having a rough week in terms of bills. Guys would ask me to dominate them, and I'd do so for a price. And now, I'd get to finally experience this once again, and there was a thrill that came out of this.

The first thing that I did, was put on the blindfold. I also cuffed his hands. He sat there, gulping. I grabbed his chin, looking him in the eyes.

"So you want me to dominate you because you're too much of a little bitch to take control? What a pathetic sight," I said.

"Ahh yes. Please mistress," he said, already getting into the role.

That's what shocked me the most about this. It was the fact that he was already so into this, and I was just beginning.

"I didn't say you should talk. You only talk when spoken to. And only when I give you permission. Got it?" I snapped at him.

"Yes mistress," he said, obedient.

"Now, what should I do with your pathetic ass first. Perhaps I should step on your pathetic dick, that you can barely use," I said.

He let out a small gasp of pleasure as I moved my leg, rubbing it there against the obvious bulge in his pants. He was hard as a rock, and it surprised me that he was like this.

"Look at you, getting hard like the dog that you are," I said.

"Yes mistress, I'm a dog," he said.

"Bark."

He let out a half-assed bark, and I smiled. I enjoyed the way that he sounded, and the pleasure that came out of this.

I smiled, moving my foot against there, pressing against his cock with a bit more force. He let out a small gasp, and I smiled.

"What's the matter? You like it when my boot is against your cock?" I asked.

"Yes mistress. Please, crush me," he said.

I put a bit more force against there, hearing him groan.

"You're too fucking loud. Clean them," I said.

I shoved my boot in his face, and he quickly went to work, cleaning off all of the edges of my boots. I laughed, watching him finally shut up as he slurped and took care of my boots, making sure that they were cleaned.

"Very good. Well, I take it that you want this mistress to take care of you, to peg your pathetic hole, and make you whimper and cry?" I asked, grabbing his chin. He nodded.

"Yes. I'm nothing more than your toy, someone that you can use as you see fit," he said.

This guy was hells getting into it. In the past I've done this with guys, but most of the time, they were usually not all that focused on the play. But this guy here was definitely into it, and there was something thrilling about that.

"Very well. If that's what you see fit, then so be it. I'll make sure you whimper and cry," I said.

"Yes mistress. Anything," he insisted.

119

There was that sound of desperation that came out of his mouth as I smiled.

I pushed him so that he was on his stomach. I got onto his back, digging my boots into there. He let out a small cry of pain, and I pushed his head down.

"You need to stay quiet, or else I'll gag you," I said.

I continued to lightly walk on him, knowing damn well that this was more than enough for him. The sounds that he made were music to my ears, making me shiver and moan with delight as I continued to move my body there, getting on top of him, enjoying the fun that came from this.

He was such a goddamn mess., this was so fun, and there was something exciting about taking over this man, making him my bitch, and watching him slowly come undone.

"What's the matter? Can't take it?" I said.

"I-I can," I heard from the muffle.

I continued to step around for a second before getting off. I walked over to the kit that I had, grabbing of course the gag and putting it into his mouth.

In truth, I just didn't want the wrong people coming in. but most therapy sessions were done for the day, so I'd get to of course, have him all to myself. That's why I kept the kit in a small corner of my office, and it looked like a regular briefcase, so it wasn't like anyone could really go and ask about that.

That's what's so thrilling about this. The fact that I could do all of this, and I had this man of all people losing his mind as I took him and teased him.

I pushed his cheeks up, pulling off his pants and boxers, revealing his large, aching cock. While I'd normally be thinking of riding that, today I wanted to make him feel good. And if this would help with well...all of the problems that he had, then so be it.

"Look at you, hard as a rock already," I told him.

"Y-yes I am mistress," he said.

"Maybe I'll milk you later on, turn you into the pathetic little slut that you are," I said.

"please mistress," he replied.

All of his sounds were muffled due to the gag but I'd been doing this long enough that I could understand just what the hell he was looking for.

But that's when I moved to my next target.

His ass.

It was right there, up in the air. It was plump, but not too big. And when I touched it, he let out a small, hissing sound of pleasure.

Look at you. Already so turned on," I said to him.

"Y-yes mistress," he said.

"As you should be. Anyways...let's make some magic," I told him.

121

I grabbed the first thing that I sued. It was a typical paddle, but on one side were little metal spikes. They of course wouldn't be that hard on the person, but for someone who was already as sensitive as he was, it would make things a bit more painful. I decided to use the flat side first, spanking him with it. He let out a small cry, enjoying the touch of my hands.

"There you go. Look at you, already losing control and turned on by the mere touches of my hands," I told him.

"Yes," he said, breathing out slightly.

I soon started to hit him again and again, enjoying the feeling of this. I soon started to watch him tense up, moaning out loud and in pleasure, and I loved everything about this sort of thing. It was fun to see him squirm, and I enjoyed it.

I continued to paddle him, switching sides at one point, the little moans only growing a little bit louder as he did this. There was something exciting about this, and I loved it. I continued to paddle and tease him, enjoying the sounds of pleasure that escaped his mouth, the fun that this brought all of us.

For a little bit, I continued to tease him, until finally, I stopped, watching his bass twitch a little bit. I then moved towards the case again, getting something a little bit harder.

"There we go," I said to him.

I grabbed the little crop that I had. This one had a much harder bite to it, and I watched his eyes widen in surprise at the feeling of this.

"Holy shit," he said pout loud as I hit him once.

"You good?"

He nodded, and I hit him a few more times with this. The little yelps and sounds that were muffled by the gag were music to my ears of course, and there was something thrilling about all of this. But I wanted more, and seeing him twitch like this was quite fun.

"Look at my little pet here. All twitching and needy," I said.

He let out a whimper, and I soon reached over, grabbing the lube and one of the plugs that I used.

"Look at your little hole. All needy for me," I said.

"Yes mistress," he muttered into the pillow. I let out a chuckle, teasing the very edge of his pucker, watching him shiver and squirm in response to my actions.

"That's right. You like this don't you? I can see you twitching and squirming like the little bitch that you are," I said, teasing the very tip of his pucker with my hand. I didn't even get far, I just knew that this alone was enough to make him lose control and composure slightly, and there was something fun about this. I loved seeing him in this state, there was something fun about this. I continued my teasing, playing with him a little bit with my finger, enough to make him shiver and squirm

123

in response to everything. He continued to let out a series of small grunts and moans, and I enjoyed hearing him like this. I continued to tease him, touching him slightly, and he soon let out a small gasp as I got right up against his pucker, moving my finger there, dancing it slightly.

"Yes," he said to himself.

I then lubed up my finger more, forcing it through there, hearing him letting out a series of small grunts and cries. He seemed to be in his own little world with this, and I loved it. I continued to touch, tease, and ply with him, watching his eyes widen, and his body react to the touches of my hand.

I loved seeing him come apart like this, and there was something at that was driving him crazy, and I wanted nothing more than to just take this whole and make him shiver and scream.

I continued to tease with one finger, and then two, then three fingers, but then I got bored. It was fun and all, but I really wanted to make him squirm, to make him really lose it.

That's when I grabbed the dildo that I had. It was only a little bit smaller than the one I used with my strap, but I pushed it in. To my surprise, it fit perfectly into his ass. I thrust it in there, giggling as I did so.

"Look at you, already turned on by this. Your ass takes so much like the little bitch it is," I said, plunging it in there. He let out a small whimper and cry, thrusting his hips upwards, enjoying the sensation of my hands there, and the toy teasing and titillating him. I then pressed the vibration function, watching him squirm there, and I couldn't help but love it. There was something thrilling about making a man like this lose it. And I was going to make him lose it and then some.

I continued the teasing for a little while, but then, I felt that urge for so much more. That crave, that need, that enticing desire for him. I soon moved the toy out of him, and I heard the little moan from his lips.

"Don't worry, you'll be filled with something even better soon," I purred.

He let out a small whimper, and I couldn't help but find this even more fun than I thought it'd be. I mean, he was here, like putty in my hands, and I couldn't help but love everything about this. It was only It was only a matter of time before I got myself together, getting the toy that I had and slowly pushing it into me. I let out a small gasp, and then, I moved towards him.

"There we go. Ready pet?" I asked.

The little whimper that I heard from him made me smile, and I felt excited about this. I soon got myself together, spreading his cheeks apart, pressing all the way into him.

I heard him tense up, and then cry out as I started plunging deep into him, watching him slowly lose all semblance of control as I moved myself deep into him. I watched his eyes widen, and the choked sobs that came out of him as I pushed myself deep within.

This was what I loved about domination. The feeling of control that this given to me through this was just…fun you know. I definitely enjoyed the feeling of this.

I began to thrust in and out, watching his body spasm in response to my touches. I then grabbed his hips, looking at him and chuckling.

"Wow, you're doing so damn well. I'm impressed with you," I told him.

He let out a small shudder, a moan of response, and I noticed his back began to arch slightly as I began to thrust in deeper and deeper, holding him there. I continued to pound him, hearing the sounds and whimpers.

I knew that he was getting close, and while it was fun just teasing him and watching him whimper, I knew that I had to end things off soonish.

I grabbed him, holding him against my body, thrusting upwards.

I grabbed his cock, milking him, and he let out a low, guttural sound, cumming against my hand. I shivered, feeling the strapon hit that one spot that made me shiver and cry out. not only after did I feel the force of my own orgasm hit me, but I pushed into him, causing him to let out a small, needy whimper of desire.

When I felt my orgasm hit me, I knew that this was definitely it. I finished up, pulling out, and I looked at him, seeing him there.

"Now you've been used my little pet. All used and neatly kept here," I said.

"Yes mistress," he said.

I soon got back to my normal type of state. While it was fun to tease him, I knew that I had to make sure I still kept an inkling of professionalism throughout all of this. I put my stuff back, took off the blindfold and gag, and I put the boots away. He laid there, still unable to say as word to me, just amazed by how good it felt. I for one didn't blame him. I mean, I knew I was good at what I did. The fact that men would come back to me even after seeing me a few times was proof alone.

But there was something else that was there, something that was bothering him.

"How are you feeling? Do you need anything?" I asked him.

He looked at me, shaking his head.

"No. not really," he admitted.

"What do you mean by that?" I asked him.

He paused, flushing crimson.

"Well it's more of...thanks for what you did. I really did like that you know," he said.

"You mean the fucking? I figured that's what you were looking for. A woman to dominate you. Consider it therapy, just don't mention it to anyone," I said.

Lord knows I'd be in deep shit if someone found out about this. William flushed, nodding.

"Yeah, I wouldn't dare. My career would be on the line. But thank you Nadine. You're kind of amazing you know," he said to me.

I flushed, nodding.

"Yeah, I feel this was good for both of us," I told him.

"Yeah, I'm really glad that I have you," he said to me.

I knew that he meant this. Deep down, everything seemed so perfect, so right, and I knew that he enjoyed this too. I sat there, thinking about the way things were.

"So I take it a part of your kisses stem from well…someone not giving you this kind of treatment?" I asked him.

"Yeah. My ex found it weird, and I never felt comfortable seeing a dominatrix about this, especially when I was with her. It was embarrassing, and I knew that it would've fixed itself so much faster if I just did. But you know how it is," he said.

"Yeah. You had the internalized desires but you were afraid of what someone else may think. I get that, and I know that you're struggling to truly understand everything. But I'm here for you, and I'm proud of you," I told him.

He nodded.

"Thank you doc. And yeah. I won't say a thing about this. But maybe we can...do this again sometime down the road?" he asked.

It was risky. He would have to sneak around, and I'd have to do the same thing just to get an inkling of this to work. But my lips curled into that of a smile.

"Sure. I wouldn't mind that. I'm sure we could arrange something good for both of us, something that benefits both parties," I told him.

The look on his face told me everything. The obvious smile, the look of pure, raw desire, and that ache that I could see in his eyes, it was so obvious that he was just as excited for this as I was.

It could be our little secret, a confidential ordeal between two people.

"Thank you. And I will make sure that this is kept under wraps," he said.

"You damn well better make sure. I know that otherwise it's not going to be good for either of us," I told him.

"You've got that right. Anyways, I hope that we can do this again. I should probably go back to work though," he said.

"Yeah, you've got a lot of people waiting on you," I admitted.

"Yeah I know. But I feel a lot better talking to you about this. Not just because of the sex. But well...everything. So thank you doctor," he said.

129

"Just call me Nadine," I replied.

His lips curled into that of a smile, one that said it all.

"Well thank you Nadine. I appreciate all that you've done for me, and everything that transpired," he replied.

I knew that he meant it. I just felt so nervous, especially given the fact that this was all happening like this. We parted ways, and while I did miss him, I knew that this was the start of something. I wasn't sure what, but I was ready to explore this.

He was the forbidden patient, the one I couldn't get out of my head.

Deeper than Mere Friendship

I waited for Jack to come over. He was my best friend, and we were going to spend the night together watching shitty horror movies and having a good time. At least, that's what he told me.

The ruth was, I wondered if there was something else there, something deeper than just the little friendship that we had. The truth was, I did have a crush on Jack, but I was scared to tell him.

I wanted to just admit it, and hope the feelings were reciprocated, but I didn't know. He'd been eying another woman, and there was something about that which set me off a little bit.

I didn't dare tell him though. That was the last thing I wanted. I didn't know what Jack thought about me, and honestly, I was scared to ask.

I heard the doorbell ring, and I quickly got myself together. I did straighten up my curly blonde hair, and put on some makeup. I opened the door, and there was Jack, with a six-pack in hand and a smile on his face.

"Hey there Vicky," he said.

"Hey! Excited for this movie night," I told him.

He grinned, but there was something about this which made me wonder things. I didn't know why. But I got a feeling that there was something different about Jack. Could not put my finger on it though.

I shrugged it off, ignoring the feeling that was there. I followed Jack inside to the living room, and as we sat on the couch together, he smiled.

"Sorry for being so late. I was kind of busy with a couple of things," he said.

"Oh it's fine. I just got everything set up," I told him.

"Great. I'm really excited for this movie night," he said.

I was too, but I also felt there was something different in the air tonight. He turned on the TV, putting in the monster movie, and soon, we began watching it.

Jack was my best friend, ever since we were kids. I felt like there was something hidden there, something missing, and I wanted to ask about it, but I didn't want to make him feel weird. But during the movie, I saw him move a little bit closer, inch by inch. I tried to ignore it, but I wondered if there was some sort of deeper meaning to that. Was he...trying to imply something? I didn't know for sure, but I felt like there was something deeper there that he refused to discuss.

When the movie was over and the credits rolled, I turned on the light. We looked at one another, the silence awkward.

'do you want me to put in another movie?" I asked him.

"Well...not really, " he said.

132

He didn't want to watch another movie? That shocked me.

"So what are you planning to do?" I asked him.

He smiled at me, a reassuring grin, and then I looked at him. He seemed different. There was obviously something else there.

"Say Vicky, you're not going to get offended if I...decide we should try something else, right?" he asked.

Something different? But Jack and I always watched movies together. Neither of us had drank a lot, so I don't know what he was getting at with this one.

That's what made me wonder.

"What the hell are you getting at Jack? What are you talking about?" I asked him.

I legit didn't know. It felt like there was some sort of embarrassing thing there that he was scared to tell me about, but he wouldn't just spit it out.

But then he flushed.

"It's a little embarrassing. Tell you what, why don't I just get the game out and if you want to play it, then great. If not, we can go back to the movies and such," he said.

I didn't know what the hell was going on. He was being so cryptic and it wasn't like him. I wanted him to just spit out whatever was bothering him, but I guess he didn't want to.

For some reason, he wanted to play the cryptic game. Well I guess two can play at that, or I'd get my answers eventually.

"Well get the game out then. We'll see what we can do," I said to him.

I didn't know what he had planned. But shortly afterwards he got out the cards. I looked at them, seeing the stick figures there.

"Deep—a game about getting to know the other person. But we're best friends Jack," I said.

"I know but...it may be fun. Something a little different from the normal bullshit, you know?" he said.

I didn't get it myself, and I thought that it was stupid, but also...I was curious. Did it have something to do with the awkwardness that Jack possessed.

"Sure, let's do this," I told him.

I wanted to find out what it was that he had planned, or even what this may mean. Jack smiled, and I felt a sudden rush of relief that he wasn't mad at me or anything.

"Good. Then it's simple. There's little cards and you put them in a few piles. There are three piles of course, and these cards determine your actions. When you get one, you can do the action, or pass, and then you have to pick another and do that action, or whatever is on the card," he said.

"And who wins?"

"Depends. I guess we'll see how this goes," he said.

I had no clue what he was trying to do with this. It seemed like a stupid ass game, and I had no clue what the endgame of any of this was. But I wanted to ease that tension that I felt in my bones, because of him. and I wanted to learn more about this.

So finally gave in, listening to him as he spread out the cards.

"I'll go first. Is that okay?" he asked.

"Y-yeah," I said, feeling my heart race.

He then grabbed a card, picking it up and reading it.

"Confess the secret that's on the tip of your tongue to them," he said.

"Is this some sort of truth or dare?" I asked Jack.

"No Vicky. It's something that has also some actions there. It brings people closer together. Well….I don't know. I'm nervous about mentioning this," he said.

"Come on man. Tell me," I told him.

He paused, flushing crimson. I didn't know why, but I felt like it had something to do with us. Something that was bigger than what we both thought.

"If I tell you…you don't plan on getting mad or anything, right?"

"Why would I get mad Jack. You've been acting weird for a bit," I said.

"Well I just want to make sure that it isn't weird or anything," he said.

I wasn't sure what was considered weird in this man's eyes. But I nodded.

"Don't worry, I'll make sure that this is all kept between us. I promise nobody else will find out about whatever it is that you are hiding," I said to him.

He looked into my eyes, obvious relief there. What was he holding back. Finally, he spoke.

"Well…what if I told you that I masturbated to you before?" he said.

I flushed. I wasn't expecting that. I mean, I thought that this was going to be him confessing he liked me or something. Which wasn't necessarily wrong. I got that vibe.

But this was different. My eyes widened, and my eyebrow raised.

"Really now," I said.

"Yeah. It was a couple of times. I feel a bit embarrassed about this," he said.

"Don't be. It's okay," I told him.

"Thanks. But yeah, I have. I guess that's a secret that I first thought about. Your turn," he said.

I picked the card, holding it.

"Give them a kiss on a body part," I read out loud.

I was red as a tomato. There was no way I was going to kiss Jack...right?"

"Well...you going to do it?" he asked me.

I looked at the options. I could get another card, and things could be worse. Or I could just do this.

"I'll take another card," I replied.

"Makes sense," he said, hiding the slight disappointment in his voice.

I took the next card, reading it out loud.

"Tell the other person a small sexy fact about yourself," I said.

God not another embarrassing one. Was this supposed to be sexual on purpose? I looked at Jack, realizing that there was no way I was getting out of this.

"Well...I have a vibrator I refuse to get rid of because it always hits that one spot. And well...I love being eaten out. my clit really likes the attention," I said.

Fuck this was embarrassing. But Jack smiled.

"What a secret. Two of them really," he teased.

I looked at him, realizing he liked this. Was this some sort of fucked up sex game that he found enjoyment in. I'd be lying if I said I didn't find this fun though. Even though it was indeed fucking embarrassing, I knew for a fact that what I was feeling definitely was a bit different.

It was both arousal, and of course…the urge for something more.

He picked the next card, reading it over.

"Kiss the other person's body part and lick it," he said.

"There's no way you're doing this, right?" I asked.

"Depends. I may want to take a risk with this. I don't want to give out more embarrassing secrets now do I?" he said.

God was this really how this was going to go? I don't know, but then I sighed.

"Fine. Where?" I asked.

"Give me your hand," he told me.

I looked at him, confused as to why he needed it, but I extended it. He grabbed my hand, kissing the tip of my finger, but then, he put the finger in his mouth, letting his tongue drag downwards against the bottom of it.

Okay that was hot. I felt my heart race, my body grow ragged with need, and a smile ghost his face once more.

"Getting kind of hot in here," he said.

"Y-yeah," I said.

Fuck it was my turn. I had no idea what in the world was going to happen. What other kinds of little secrets were there? I looked around, and then, I picked up the next card.

"Show your genitals to the other person," I said.

Was he fucking serious? I looked at Jack, and he smiled.

"If you're nervous about this, I can do this with you," he told me.

That only made things worse. The little crush that I had was starting to become more and more apparent. Did this guy just like teasing me like this? I wanted the answers, but then, I sighed.

"Fine. I'll do it," I said.

I started to undo my pants, sliding them off, and then, I removed my underwear.

I shaved, not because I thought this would be happening, but because I imagined it was getting a bit hairy and unkempt. He looked over, nodding.

"Very nice," he said.

"Don't make this embarrassing. Please," I told him.

"I'm not. In fact, I'll also hold up my end and show you," he said. He pulled his pants down, revealing his erection.

I immediately blushed. He was huge, fucking packing, and I knew that it would feel amazing inside me. but I didn't want to mention that.

And it didn't help that he was hard as a rock too. Fuck this was making the game even more awkward for the two of us.

"W-wow," I said.

"Not bad huh?" he teased.

"Yeah. Not at all," I told him, struggling to form words as I looked at the meaty member. This was getting harder to concentrate on. But I had to keep my wits about me, no matter what.

"Anyways, it's your turn," I finally said, putting everything aside.

I looked at him, and he grabbed a card.

"Stick a finger inside the other person," he said.

"Are you fucking serious?"

"Hey, I could just stick it in your ear if I wanted to," he joked.

I knew he wouldn't do that though. This was all a game, and this was making me lose it right then and there. I started to flush as he brought the finger closer to my pussy, spreading me apart as he plunged it in.

I let out a small cry. He just had to stick it in, but then he began to explore, fingering it. I felt my eyes roll to the back of my head, my body suddenly crave more of the touch, and the ache and pleasure that came out of this was only driving me crazier and crazier.

He continued to tease me, plunging his fingers deep into my pussy, and it was driving me mad., I started to feel my whole body tense up, the sudden feeling of my pussy begin to tighten, and I let out a small cry.

He pulled it out, licking it, looking me in the eyes with a surprised look.

"Wow, I didn't know you'd cum that fast," he said.

"I-it wasn't like I meant to be," I told him.

"Relax. Trust me, I know this game is helping us discover things. Just take it easy. Besides, it's your turn," he said.

I looked at him, still flushing from what had just occurred, and I grabbed the next card. This one was a lot easier than well the last few that I had.

"Lick their nipples," I said.

I looked at Jack, who weas laughing.

"That should've been mine," he said.

"Well it wasn't. I guess I can do that now," I told him.

I leaned in, taking the tip of one of the nipples into my mouth, sucking on the flesh there, making me suddenly feel hot and bothered by this. The groan that came out of his mouth made me feel turned on, in ways that I didn't expect. I started to suck and tease on it, flicking my tongue against the very tip of this, moving my other hand towards the other nipple, teasing it.

"Okay...I think that's more than enough," he said.

I did get lost in the teasing, turned on by the way that this felt. I looked at the cards. At this point, I felt like it was just a waste of time that this happened. I looked at them, and then he grabbed a card.

"Give them a kiss," he read.

"You mean like...."

141

"Yeah, a kiss-kiss," he said.

Well we were already half naked, and after what had just happened, I didn't think this game would be of much use for far too much longer.

"I guess...he goes nothing," I told him.

"Yeah. Here goes nothing," he said to me.

He leaned in, and we soon kissed slightly. At first, it was an awkward kiss, one that had a little bit of chastity to it, but then moments later, we both deepened the kiss, enjoying the feeling of one another, and the passion that this ignited.

I loved the way that this felt, and it was clear that he did too. We continued to make out for what felt like forever, and it was definitely making me lose my mind, making me want more from him.

We kissed for what felt like forever until he pulled away, looking me in the eyes.

"I don't think we need to play this game anymore," he said.

"What do you mean?"

"Well...we're kind of like this. Do you want to continue it?" he asked.

I mean I did. There was that ache inside of me that craved this. I soon nodded.

"Yeah, I'd love that," I told him.

He beamed, an obvious smile on his face.

"Good. Because I want that too," he said.

I grabbed another card, holding it there.

"Try missionary together," I said.

"I mean, we cand o that, but let's get to that point first. I want...I want to kiss you again," he said to me.

"You sure?" I asked. I didn't expect this to happen so suddenly with my best friend of all people. But he nodded.

"Yeah. I'd be lying if I didn't feel the same way about you Vicky. I brought this over because I thought it would be funny. But it's kinda...made me realize how much I fucking want you," he said to me.

I blushed crimson. I mean, I didn't want this to affect our friendship, but I didn't think it would do that. At least, that's not the vibes I was getting from this one.

"Are you sure? I don't want to make this weird for anyone," I said to him.

"No. I like this. I like you," he told me.

I beamed, and soon, we pressed our lips to one another, kissing passionately, enjoying the feeling of one another. This stupid little sex game ended up changing our lives forever, and it made me realize that there were unbridled feelings deep within me, that threatened to come the fuck out.

We continued to kiss for what felt like forever and soon, before I knew it, I felt a tongue snake out, meeting my own. This was different from earlier. There were any holds back anymore. I continued to kiss and make out with him, enjoying the touch that this made me feel, enjoying everything that came out of this. For a long time, we simply made out here enjoying one another, when finally, he pushed me into the couch.

"Now I get to see the rest of you," he told me.

I shivered, moaning slightly at the way his voice sounded. It was low and guttural and there was something about it which made me lose control, and there was clearly that need that only grew more so, and that unbridled need for one another.

He kissed down my neck, touching every single part of this, and as he kissed down every part of my neck, I started to shiver and cry out.

I loved this, and I knew that there was clearly a desire for more, a need that was unbridled, and that ache which made me shiver with delight.

He soon moved his lips to my collarbone, biting down on the flesh, making a small hickey appear there. I cried out, looking at him with mild annoyance.

"I didn't say to leave Marks," I muttered.

"Sorry, I just thought that your neck looked nice," I heard him say to me.

I flushed, but then nodded.

"Yeah, it is nice," I said.

"I just want to make you feel good. Because...you mean a lot to me Vicky," he said.

I blushed, and nodded.

"Yeah, you mean a lot to me too," I told him as well.

There was clearly a bit of tension that went along with this, and I felt embarrassed even admitting it, but he seemed to understand and there was something about the way that he treated me which made me feel better too.

He soon started to move his hands towards my shirt, pulling it off, grasping my breasts from over the confines of the bra.

"Wow," he said.

"You know you can take off the bra you know," I said.

"Yeah, I know. Let me have this moment please," he said.

He touched my breasts, massaging them, and even with the bra on, I moaned. There was something nice about a pair of hands that weren't your own touching, teasing, and playing with your titties. There was something exciting about the little touches too, and I couldn't help but enjoy the presence, and the moment that this gave me.

For a long time, he simply played with them, moving his hands to the back of my bra, pulling on the clasp, undoing this and letting them come out of the confines.

145

I shivered, moaning in pleasure as I started to feel his hands there, touching and playing with them. His hands moved towards my nipples, playing with them. I cried out, feeling my hands grip the couch as I felt the small, subtle touches. There was something different about these touches. They were nice, but I also could feel how close I was to losing it right then and there.

His hands moved against each of the tips of my nipples, pulling and tugging on them. I cried out, moaning as I bucked my hips upwards, shivering with delight at every single touch that came out of this. I started to feel his hands continue to move, touch, and tease there, and it was already driving me mad. I didn't know how much more of this I could take.

But then, his lips replaced one of the hands, touching the tip of it with small, subtle licks. The little licks and teases right then and there was enough to drive me insane. I let out a small moan, excited and turned on by this. He continued to lick and suck, pleasuring me there, and I lost all semblance of reality as I continued to feel this.

There was something thrilling about the way that he touched me, about the way that he teased me, and I couldn't help but feel like I was slowly coming undone. He flicked his tongue there, tugging on the other nipple, causing it to harden in response to his actions. I let out a cry, begging for more, aching for him.

That's when he pulled back, smiling at me, moving between my legs and pushing two fingers inside. His thumb moved right over the clit, just barely touching and teasing me there. I didn't know how much of this I could take. I wanted more, and I ached for him. I knew that I was close already, and that he knew this too.

He continued the teasing, every single motion and touch driving me crazy. After a brief second though, he pulled my hips upwards, his tongue coming out, exploring every part of me, touching my folders, teasing the nub of my clit, sucking on that.

I cried out, feeling my body instantly react to this. There was something about his lips that made me almost lose it there. I let out a guttural sound, one that was barely understood or distinguished, but I held onto the couch, moaning in response to his touches, his licks, and the sucking and pleasuring of every part of the flesh that he had.

That was something that I enjoyed. It was something that I ached and wanted to feel, that I desired more than anything else, and I knew that he was also getting into it in the same vein that I was. I knew that I was already close to my limit, enjoying the pleasure that came out of this.

He then pushed his tongue, exploring inside of me, pressing against each part of the moment, and it made me suddenly start to tense holding the couch.

But as soon as I felt the sudden onset of the orgasm hit me, it was gone. He pulled his mouth away, causing me to pout in response to his actions.

"Dammit," I muttered.

"Hey, I wasn't going to let you get away with that that easily," he teased.

"You motherfucker," I told him.

"I know that you enjoy this," he replied.

I rubbed Jack's blonde hair, looking into his blue eyes. He then moved himself so that his cock was right at my entrance.

I was nervous to say the least. I had no clue how this was going to feel, or if it would be good. But I wanted to trust him. I wanted this to be okay. and then, moments later, he pushed himself inside.

I cried out, feeling my whole body get filled up in an instance as I felt his cock all the way inside of there, buried within me. I felt my whole body suddenly tense up, and the moans that escaped my mouth drive me crazy. I began to hold onto the couch, moving my hips against him, letting out a series of cries.

This was so good, although he was filling me up pretty tightly. It did feel a little uncomfortable, but I didn't mind it. I started to feel his thrusts grow stronger, and as he looked into my eyes, I knew that there was that implicit desire for more, that need for all of this, and I couldn't help but feel the same way.

But then I stopped, looking over at the cards.

"Grab another," I said with a teasing smile.

He was confused, but then he did so.

"Get on top," he said.

"Don't mind if I do," I replied.

I pushed him down onto the couch, scrambling on top of him. when I finally got there, we locked eyes, my brown eyes looking into his blue ones, and there was clearly a feeling of excitement and need which came out of this too.

"There we go," I said.

I slid down on his cock, moaning as I felt him suddenly grip me, moving his cock deep in and out of me, making me shiver with delight, enjoying the feeling of all of this. There was something nice about this, something thrilling, and I wanted nothing more than to just enjoy the moment, embrace it, and love every single moment of this.

For a long time, I moved up and down. Then, two hands came forward, teasing my breasts, touching the tips of my nipples there, making me lose all semblance of control, enjoying the feel of the moment, the pleasure that came out of this, and the sounds of our bodies together.

It was a thrill that I didn't expect to enjoy so much, but when we locked eyes, there was clearly that unbridled desire that need for one another, and that need for more.

After a few more thrusts, he pulled me down, kissing me passionately as his fingers moved towards my clit, rubbing there, making me cry out, and then, he pulled my lips to his own, kissing me passionately.

For a second, we just kissed. He finished, and I suddenly felt my whole body lose it. I cried out, my orgasm hitting me to the core. I suddenly moved back, arching, and then, I finished.

When we were done, we looked at one another, neither of us saying a word for a moment. There was clearly something that needed to be said, but neither of us knew how to go about saying this.

All I knew was that Jack changed me. my best friend, someone who was always there by my side, now wanted...something more. And there was that feeling of desire, a need to also take the plunge and do this.

"Wow," I said to him as I moved out of him, sitting there. I grabbed a morning after pill and took it. I had one just in case. Never thought I'd use it in this situation.

When we got back to the couch, I sat next to him and tried to figure out what to say. Then, he spoke.

"You know I've wanted that for a while," he admitted.

"You mean like....for both of us," I asked him.

"Yeah. I've liked you for a long time Vicky. I just didn't want to make things weird. I brought this over to see what may happen. Maybe some sex games could help determine this. I never thought that it'd be something like that though," he said to me.

I didn't expect it either. I simply nodded, surprised by this.

"Yeah, you and me both," I told him.

"Anyways, I guess it's safe to say that it was a lot of fun, and I enjoyed that," he told me.

"Yeah, I did as well," I told him.

We looked at one another, and then for a long time, we didn't say a word. Finally, he sighed, trying to grapple with the obvious feelings that he had.

"Would you be against dating though? I didn't want to push my luck or anything, but if you'd like, we could—"

"I'd like that," I said. It was something I hadn't really thought all that much about, but now that we were here, in this moment together, there was clearly a desire for more, a desire for something together. He then nodded.

"Thank god you feel the same way. I was a little worried you didn't feel this way," he said.

"No I do. I'm really happy to have this chance though," I said.

"Me too. I didn't think it's work out like this. But it did, and I'm glad about that," he said.

"I am too," I replied.

I didn't think I was in love with him, but there was clearly a desire for more. As we kissed one another, I eagerly accepted this, enjoying the touch of his lips, and of him.

151

we stayed like this for a long time, enjoying the touch of one another, and I knew that this was what I wanted to.

That night, he spent the night, even though we hadn't done that before. But I knew for a fact that Jack changed my feelings, made me realize what I'd been missing out on, and I knew that this was the beginning of something new, amazing, and something better than ever expected it to be.

I had a good feeling about the future, and about the desires which showed through that night, and brought us forward.

Her new Farmhands

"So you're the new ones?" I asked the two guys that walked on in.

They stepped over to me, smiling with little wry smiles.

"Sure am! My name is Toby," the blonde guy said.

"I'm Kenneth," the other guy, a tall, muscular guy with brown hair and subtle stubble on their faces said.

My eyes glazed over them, and I smiled in slight excitement.

"Yeah, my name's Mary. My dad hired you guys. But he'll be gone for the next week or so. So I'll be the one in charge for a bit," I said.

My name is Mary Lindback. My dad Craig Lindback owns this huge-ass dairy farm. Usually he'd run the whole thing himself but well...things don't always go as planned.

My dad ended up falling and breaking his leg. Shit hit the fan, and while I tried to keep up with everything, and my dad was a stubborn ass and continued to work, the doctor said he needed to take off some time, at least a week or two in order to recover so he didn't fuck up his leg further.

That of course led to my mom taking him to one of the nearby towns, where he'd get a "vacation" of sorts for a little bit. My mom insisted he take some damn time off, and it was obvious that he needed it.

But of course my dad is a stubborn ass, and I'd have to run the farm by myself. He told me he sent over some hands to help me with this. I was expecting family. Not two attractive guys that I never met till this point.

"Well….I guess it's time to get started then. I thought that your dad would be here. But I guess he really did hurt himself. Not just a rumor," Kenneth said.

"Well yeah, my dad doesn't fuck around with this. He's stubborn, so of course, if he ends up stopping his job, it's for a good reason," I said.

"Indeed. Anyways, can you show us around so we can get started? We'd love to help with some of the fields and such. It's a big ass farm. Can't believe he was doing this all on his own," Toby said.

"Yeah, I heard your dad was stubborn, but not like this," Kenneth added.

"Yeah well, he's gone so I've got to take care of this place. Anyways, my dad had it set up so you can stay in the guest house and such," I said.

Of course, in the bowels of my mind, I had an idea. I thought about…possibly letting them stay with me. but I didn't want things to get weird like that. It was the first time I'd been left alone like this, and I didn't want to fuck things up.

The truth was, my dad was a bit of straightedge, so that meant I rarely had the freedom to do what I wanted. And the fact that I was given this chance both excited me, and made me wonder how much of this I could get away with. I liked the idea of him possibly letting me do more, but also...I didn't know what else would happen now that well...we were here like this.

But I couldn't stop thinking about them. They were attractive as well, hot guys that I'd have to work with on the farm with. I moved my hands over to the guest house, grabbing the key and handing them over to them.

"Here you are," I told them.

"Well thanks," Kenneth said.

When our hands touched, I flushed crimson. I shouldn't be getting this excited over shit like this, but here we fucking were. I flushed thinking about the state of everything, and what this would mean for me. but then, moments later, I heard Kenneth speak,.

"Anyways, we can start with the farm work around here. If you want to show us anything, we can do it," he said.

I looked at the different places. They had to know at least a little bit about where the equipment was before I could let them on their own.

"Let me show you around the place a little bit. Fi that's okay of course," I told them.

"Sure as shit is. I'm glad we have such a cute guide like yourself," toby added with a wink.

I felt the heat burst through my body. I knew already these two would get me in so much trouble. But also...my parents weren't here, so it's not like they'd berate me or anything. If anything, they probably didn't care. Then again, they were kind of traditional.

But I was nineteen. I was old enough to make decisions like this on my own, so the prospect of having these two so close didn't feel like it was an accident. I mean, if my dad didn't want me to get into shit like this, they could've just had Billy come over. He's my cousin and a total oaf, but gets the work done.

But no...they did this. On purpose, and that made me realize the state of everything, and what was going on.

After a little bit of thinking, I walked with the two of them over to different parts of the farm, showing them how to use the milking machines.

"You sure know how to milk, don't you?" Kenneth said.

"Course. I'm an expert with milking," I teased.

I saw his eyes move down between my chest, and I flushed, putting my hands there.

"I mean...I've used them a lot," I said.

I felt like a fucking moron saying shit like that. I mean, how could I sound any more pathetic. But then....I heard them laugh. Instead of being upset, they laughed at my dumbass shit.

"No it's okay. I like that you know so much about milking. Very interesting," Toby said.

"Y-yeah," I replied, flushing crimson at the idea of this. For a long time, I didn't say anything, but then, I sighed.

"Anyways, I guess we should get started with this. I'll feed them while you guys make sure they're properly rounded up," I said to them.

"We can do that. We're good with wrangling," Toby said.

"Yeah, it's something fun we like to do," Kenneth said.

"I'm sure you're experts on wrangling," I teased.

That's when I flushed, realizing how sexual this was getting. I flushed at the realization of this. I knew that this flirting would get me in trouble eventually, but not like this.

However, I enjoyed the playful flirting that went on with these two. There was something fun about flirting with them that made it even more adventurous and fun. For a long time, we simply continue this flirting.

Over the next couple of days, I felt their eyes stare at me a little longer than usual. I flushed, realizing that they enjoyed this as much as I did. I liked it though, feeling like it was obvious that they were enjoying this as much as I was.

But I didn't want to make any weird moves or anything that would get me in trouble. After all, they were here for my dad, not for me of course.

But one day, I was working in the barn, getting the hay out. However, it was up on the top area of the barn. As I reached up to grab it, the little stool I was using to reach the top started to shake. I held myself, bracing myself for impact, when suddenly, I fell into something soft. I looked over, seeing Kenneth there, holding me in his arms.

"T-thanks for that," I said, turning as red as a tomato.

"You're most welcome. Don't want you to get hurt, right?" he said.

He was definitely correct about that. Didn't need two people in the Lindback family hurt.

"Anyways, I think I'll be going," I said, rushing out of there.

That night, when I laid in bed, I moved my hands between my legs, teasing my entrance. I let out a small sigh, pushing my hands deep into her. For a long time, I started to push them inside, two fingers, imagining it being Kenneth's dick inside of me. as I did that, I thumbed my clit, letting out a small sigh as I thought about toby against my breasts, teasing them while I was fucked.

"Ahh," I said, feeling my hips jerk forward. I began thrusting faster, touching myself, imagining them there, when suddenly, I heard the sound of rustling. I looked upwards, seeing that there was a shadow there.

Was it them? A part of me felt embarrassed if so, but if they ran into me during this, I certainly couldn't help but enjoy this. I didn't know what to say to them though if I did find them there.

One moment passed before I thought about it...about possibly seeing what they were up to. But I stopped myself.

I didn't want to seem like a desperate fuck or anything.

Over the next few days, I started to work closely with both Toby and Kenneth. They were interesting guys, not just two people my dad hired, and we were close.

"Say, do you guys want to come over for dinner tonight? I normally make it for my parents but...they're not here right now," I offered.

It may seem weird to some people, but I did enjoy taking care of people. They looked at one another and then nodded.

"I'd love to. I just don't want to be a damn bother or anything," Kenneth said.

"Oh you're far from that. In fact, you're a welcome distraction," I said to them.

They looked at one another, and then at me. we went back over to my place, where I had the dinner set up, and as we all sat down to eat, I could see their eyes lingering upon me.

"You guys like the food?" I asked.

"Yes. It's amazing. Definitely really good," Kenneth said.

I have to admit, you're certainly a star in the kitchen. You're not just fun to milk with," toby said.

I flushed realizing he meant something else. I then spoke.

"Yeah I try to be," I told them.

"Anyways, let's dig on in and finish up dessert. We had a long ass day," Kenneth said.

The conversation changed back to food, but I could sense the tension that was there, just screaming to finally come out. when all of this was said and done, they sat back, sighing.

"That was good," Kenneth said.

"Sure was. My compliments to Mary here though. She's amazing, and definitely handy in the kitchen," Toby said.

"Oh shucks. I'm just trying to give everyone a nice little experience. And I mean...you guys have helped a lot with all of the farm work around here. Kind of sucks it won't last forever," I told them.

"Indeed. By the way, any word on your dad coming back?" Kenneth asked.

"He said as early as tomorrow evening, but I doubt it," I said to them. I didn't think he'd come back that fast. But my dad is also a stubborn motherfucker, so I wouldn't be surprised.

That's when I saw their faces change. A smile ghosted Toby's face, and Kenneth nodded.

"Very well. Good to know. It makes things a bit easier for both of us then," he said.

"What do you mean?" I asked. I had no idea what they had planned, or even what they proposed to do.

They looked at one another, smiling excitedly, before moving towards me, looking me in the eyes.

"What's going on then guys?" I asked them.

"Oh, we wanted to give you a little present for all of the hard work. You're definitely a great boss Mary," Kenneth said.

"What do you mean?" I asked.

That's when it happened. I felt Kenneth's lips press against my own. I kissed him, feeling my body tense for a second, surprised that he even wanted this, but then I slowly relaxed. Kissing him felt nice. He had soft lips, and despite his rugged personality, I had a feeling I wouldn't be able to get enough of this if I wasn't careful.

For a long time, I started to feel my body grow nervous, but I also liked the feeling of his lips against my own, of the touch that was there, and as I kissed him, I relaxed, enjoying the sensation of it all. For a bit, we just stayed there kissing and exploring one another's lips.

But then, toby grabbed my chin, turning me so that I could face him, and then, our lips moved and touched against one another. His kisses were a bit more passionate, which surprised even me, making me shiver with delight and enjoy the feeling of all of this. For a bit, we stayed like this, and I didn't mind the excitement, need and desire that came out of this too. For a bit, we continued to make out, and then, shortly afterwards, he pulled back.

"But...why?" I asked them. I mean they were both super attractive, but I didn't know they felt the same way about me. did they?

"We wanted to give you a little something to remember us by. Especially if we have to leave tomorrow. You're pretty cute Mary, and good at milking," Kenneth said.

"Indeed. We wanted to make this fun for everyone, and Kenneth and I spoke. We thought about...giving you a fun time if that's what you're into. We can show you many things, since we know quite a bit," Toby purred.

I knew exactly what they were getting at, and I felt a little nervous about this. But then I nodded.

"Yeah. I'd like that," I told them.

They beamed, leaning in and giving me a kiss, staying like this and enjoying the sensation of the touch, the pleasure that came out of this, and for a second, I couldn't help but enjoy the touch and passion that came from it.

They then grabbed my waist, and Kenneth pulled me into his arms, carrying me bridal-style up the stairs to the bedroom I had. I was surprised that they knew where to go, but I guess they just assumed.

When they got up there, Kenneth put me on the bed, giving me a long, passionate kiss. I immediately melted into this, kissing him back, enjoying the feeling of this.

His tongue snaked out, and I soon moved my own tongue to meet his, enjoying the sensation of everything that came out of this.

For a bit, we simply stayed like this, and I enjoyed the sensation of it too. But then moments later, he started to move down my body, kissing and touching my neck with the slightest of touches.

I purred, shivering with delight, enjoying the sensation of this. He soon lightly nibbled on my neck there. As Kenneth did this, toby moved his lips, brushing them against my own, and I quickly kissed him back, enjoying the feeling of his own lips. His were a bit rougher than Kenneth's, a different sensation, and there was something thrilling about the different touches, the feelings of such, and the pleasure that came out of this.

I soon started to move my hips, feeling that urge, that need, and that desire that started to push through me, making me enjoy this too.

I began to feel their lisp descend down my body, lightly touching and teasing the sides of my neck, pressing against there and nibbling on the flesh. I tensed up, bucking my hips and moving slightly, feeling the force and pleasure that came out of this drive me to the point of madness.

I enjoyed it, and I enjoyed the feeling of such. It was amazing, and it made me excited for a lot of things, and as he continued to press his lips towards the crook of my neck, biting and teasing the flesh there, I felt my whole body give in, and the pleasure grow.

I was enthralled. I was completely immersed in the feelings that came over me with this. I started to feel Kenneth's tongue move down further and further, nibbling in the wake of his touches, and then, before I knew it, he got in between my breasts, biting on my collarbone before he started to move his hands downwards, teasing the very tip of the fabric of my shirt.

Then, there was toby, who bit down against that part of my neck, lightly nibbling and touching the flesh there making me shiver and cry out with delight, enjoying the feeling of such. I then felt him press his lips there deeper and deeper, enjoying the sounds that came out of my lips.

He then moved towards the other part of the sweater, pulling it over my head.

Kenneth's hands were the first ones to explore my body, touching my breasts and teasing them from outside the cups. I shivered, moaning, and then toby's own hands moved to the tip of my nipple, playing with it there watching my eyes widen and my hips begin to move forward.

"Fuck," I said out loud, enjoying the feeling of this, loving the sensation that came with the touches. The little ghosts of touches against my breasts, nipples, and everything else made me enjoy the feeling, completely enraptured in the pleasure of the moment, and the delight that I felt.

For a long time, I just simply moaned, feeling like it was just taking over me. I wanted nothing more than to just completely lose control, to enjoy everything, and that's when I felt their hands move to the back of my bra, undoing the clasp, pulling it off, and my breasts came out of there.

I had a pretty sizable chest, so when they were exposed, I let out a small gasp, feeling a flush ghost my face. I moved my hand into my red hair, teasing the very edges of this, playing with the fringe there, and I looked at them, my eyes wide with lust and need.

Kenneth was the first to act, touching the very tip of my nipple, playing with them against his hand. As he did that, I suddenly felt my body grow hot, and I knew that this was something that I craved. He touched the very edge, causing the nipple to harden. As he did that, I felt toby's lips against the other nipple, touching it there. As they continued to tease and service me, I started to feel my whole body ache, growing strongly, and I felt like there was something more brewing within.

I started to feel the heat grow from within, touching and teasing every single aspect of them, enjoying the feeling of such. Both of them groaned as they heard my sounds, the little cries and moans of pleasure which came out of my mouth. It was then when, after a few more moments, Kenneth's hands moved towards both, teasing the very edges, making me shiver with delight, crying out loud, enjoying the feeling of all of this as time began to pass forward.

I ached for them. There was that deep-seated need for both of them to take me like this, and I knew that they enjoyed the feeling of this too. I could see them looking

165

at me, the eyes of need obvious. Then, I felt their hands move downwards, until of course they got between my legs, touching the heat that was there against my jeans.

As they did so, I tensed up, moaning out loud and enjoying the feeling of this. The little touches against the heat of my entrance were only making my heart beat faster and faster, the ache and need growing within. They were just touching me slowly, making me feel turned on and teased from this. I was excited for more, and I craved more.

A pair of hands moved towards my jeans, touching them and then looking into my eyes. I simply nodded, needing them to do this, and then, I felt their hands slide the jeans off my body, getting them over my ass until they were down and then off to the side.

I shivered, realizing that this was the beginning of something more. I soon felt another hand move towards my clit, rubbing it from the outside. When I felt that I jumped, flushing.

"You okay there?" Toby asked.

"Yeah sorry. Just…a bit sensitive down there you know," I said with a blush.

"It's all good. I'll make sure that you're taken care of properly then," he said.

The reassurance in his voice made me smile, but not before he rubbed there, touching and teasing, and then, he started to move his hand to my panties, sliding them off. When his thumb encircled the clit, I shivered, moaning out loud, completely enraptured in the pleasure of the moment, the feeling this gave me, and everything good that came out of this. He continued to tease, every single little touch driving me crazy, and I loved the way that this felt too.

For a long time, they just teased, and I felt a finger dip into me. it was large, and it filled me up. While toby did this, Kenneth moved towards my nipples, pressing his lips to them, teasing and touching them, making me lose all semblance of control and ache that grew within me.

They continued this, and for a long time, I felt like I was at my limit, that aching need driving me crazy, and I wanted to just lose it. But I was so close to the edge, and the two fingers that were within me started to move around, pressing up against that spot.

I was so close, I didn't know how much more of this I could take! But as soon as It happened, they pulled back, making me shiver.

"Come on, I need it," I said.

"You will get it. You've done this before, right?" Toby asked.

I shook my head, red as a tomato as they looked at me with widened eyes.

"You guys are my firsts. But I have...used toys and shit before," I said.

167

I wasn't a total virgin per se, but this would be a new experience for me. They looked at one another, smiling in excitement, and then looked back at me.

"Well then I guess it's safe to say that we'll be having a lot of fun with this," Kenneth said.

"We sure as shit will be," Toby added.

I flushed, but then nodded.

"Good. I'm excited for this," I told them.

"Yes, we'll make sure everything's properly taken care of then," Toby said.

He pushed another finger inside, making me gasp out in surprise, but as they pumped into me, I knew that I was getting to my limit.

He pulled back, making sure I was okay before reaching into his pocket, grabbing a condom and slipping it onto his cock.

It was much bigger than I thought it'd be, but I wasn't going to let that get me down. I looked into his eyes, and he nodded.

"There we go. That's good," he said to me.

As I watched him spread me apart, I started to flush. I knew it'd be big, but I didn't realize that he'd be so large. As he slid into me I closed my eyes, bit my lip, and then gasped as he got all the way inside me.

Toby looked me in the eyes, to make sure he was fine, and I nodded.

"Yes. Please keep going," I insisted.

I wanted to feel more of him, to feel him deep within me. He soon started to push in and out, pressing in deeply, holding me there as I looked into his eyes, letting out a small moan of pleasure as we started to hold one another. For a long time, I started to hold onto him, feeling the pleasures of the moment, the ache and excitement which came from me, and then, after a few more moments, I felt something against my lips.

It was Kenneth. His cock was there, big and thick, twitching as I looked at it. I flushed, but then I opened my mouth, accepting him completely. I felt him push into my mouth, filling me up, making me shiver with delight, enjoying the sensation of this, feeling him groan as he pushed into my mouth. I suddenly felt his cock against the back of my throat, and I started to hold back from gagging, simply because I didn't want that embarrassment. But it felt nice., I liked how they used me, even though I felt a little bit nervous.

A pair of hands moved to my thighs, grasping them, holding them against their shoulders, and then I felt toby's cock deep within me. I shivered, crying out loud, enjoying the feeling of this. He gripped my thighs, holding them there as he pushed in deep, enjoying the feeling of my body against his. I moaned, completely enraptured by the feeling of his lips, moaning with need and desire, the ache and pleasure of it all driving me crazy.

For a long time, they continued this, each of them taking my holes, pushing in deep, causing me to feel a newfound pleasure. Then, I felt a pair of hands move towards my nipples, teasing the edges of them, making me shiver and cry out loud, completely immersed in the feelings of this. For a moment, they continued, and then, I felt something against my clit, lightly rubbing there. The smallest of touches made my body tense, and made me let out a small groan of pleasure, the aching need driving me crazy.

For a moment, they held me there, each of them keeping my holes properly taken care of, when suddenly, I felt toby push against me, a hand move to my clit to rub against me, and then he groaned, filling me with his seed.
as he did that, he touched against that one spot. As he did so, I cried out, holding onto him, and then I suddenly released, the pleasure of the moment driving me insane.

For a long time, I didn't move. Then, a pair of hands moved to my head, pushing me in. what surprised me next was Kenneth's' seed.

It filled up my mouth, causing me to let out a gagging sensation. But I didn't want to spit it out. I kept it down, swallowing everything, enjoying the feeling of this as it flooded my mouth. For a long time, after Kenneth finished, he didn't move. We all stayed like this, all of us surprised by how good this felt, and the pleasure we all experienced.

It was a different feeling to say the least, and while I was a bit surprised myself, I certainly wasn't against it either.

After a brief moment, they pulled back and I sat there, completely amazed by how good this felt, the pleasure that they provided to me, and the excitement that came with it.

"Wow," I told them.

"You good?" Toby asked.

"More than good. That was just…wow. I should've asked you guys to bone me sooner," I replied.

It was something on the back of my mind, but I didn't realize just how utterly amazing this was going to feel. Both Kenneth and toby looked at one another, and then at me, surprised by the way I felt.

"Well I enjoyed this just as much as you did," Kenneth said.

"Yeah, me too," Toby replied.

I smiled.

"Yeah, I'm really glad that I got to share this moment with both of you," I admitted.

It was an exciting feeling, that's for sure, and I knew that there was a desire for more. I then moved, pushing my breasts together and smiling.

"Well, if you guys want to stick around for a bit, I'm sure that you can. I don't think my dad will be coming back tonight," I purred.

That's what excited me. I was alone with both of them, and they liked it just as much. They both beamed, looking at one another, and then at me.

"Well since you're asking so nicely, I certainly wouldn't mind it," Toby purred.

"Me too. We can keep this our little secret," Toby said.

I beamed, moving towards them, rubbing their cocks. They both groaned, hard once again, and I licked my lips.

I got between them, licking, teasing, and playing with their cocks. These two introduced me to a newfound life, something that I'd never experienced up till this point, and I couldn't help but enjoy it. I liked the idea of these two simply taking me, playing with me, pleasuring me completely. And I had a feeling that they enjoyed this too.

And that of course wasn't to say that they were going to deny this either. They wanted this as much as I did, and for the rest of the night, we were making love, feeling one another's bodies, and enjoying each other.

To say that this was a small little instance would be wrong. It awoke something in all of us. The next evening, my dad came home, asking me how things were. I of course told them it was great, and that the guys were a huge help.

"Do you think we could keep them around for a bit?" I asked him.

He pursed his lips, and then nodded.

"I think that could be arranged," he said.

I gave my dad an innocent smile, but of course, I knew what would come with this. We had a pretty good relationship already, the three of us, and this would only make things even better.

"Thanks dad," I said.

And that's how it began. How my dad hired two farmhands, and we ended up having quickies behind the barn while he was busy. My dad never found out, and it would be the secret I'd take to my grave, never telling a soul about.

The Billionaire's Secret

No way.

There was no way in hell that this was happening.

But as I read the contents of the message, my fingers shook, my body suddenly tightened, and a feeling of dread hit me.

I know your secret Amy. I know everything. And you'll need to keep me quiet. You know where to find me.

I knew who this was from.

That rat bastard Cody.

Cody was a guy that I knew from my college days, someone who I didn't want to ever remember. But unfortunately, I was in this shithole of a mess, unable to get out of this.

He knew my secret about the partying.

Little old me, perfectly innocent billionaire Amy Sanders was now at risk for being exposed. The innocent arc and attitude was there on purpose, and now...I had to worry about this bullshit.

That fucking dick! I didn't know what to do about any of this. I couldn't even tell my friends. The only people who knew about my clubbing and hobbies were of course my friends :Stacy and Stephanie, but they also weren't part of the elites.

That meant that if this was exposed, I'd be fucked.

"What do I do...." I told myself.

I had no idea what to say to him, or even what to respond with. Cody was of course, one of the rival billionaires and the son of my father's biggest rival Travis Gibbons.

Cody Gibbons always loved to create a shitload of trouble, no matter what it might be, and that of course was something that I hated, and something I very much disliked.

I wanted to cry. If this word got out...I'd be royally fucked, that's for sure. I guess the best thing for me to do at this time would be to find out if there was any way for me to keep this a secret.

If the press found out about this, it'd hurt my dad, and I didn't want that. My dad was a big part of my life, my rock. And to know that he was in danger because of this man...royally pissed me the hell off.

That's why I needed to handle this all in private. I didn't want to put my dad's company at risk.

But how do you begin with something like this? Where does someone begin? I can't necessarily threaten the bastard. He's the one who has me by the balls for fucks sake.

Or it would be tits in this case, since I'm a girl.

I knew where Cody lived. He was at a private home that was somewhat close to his dad's place. He somewhat ran the company, but not as much as his dad did. Either way, I'd be meeting him on his own turf, and I don't know how to feel about that.

I guess the proper response was worried? I don't really know how to feel about this, other than of course, worried about the future, and about what may transpire out of this.

The best thing for me to do of course, was to play it by ear, and of course to hope for the best., I didn't know what to tell him, other than to not fucking expose that or else.

What did he want from me though? I hope it wouldn't be something bad.

I sighed, heading out of my dad's place and making my way over to the car. As I went by, my dad asked me if anything was wrong. To which I flashed him a fake smile.

"Everything's okay dad. Trust me on this," I lied.

But I had to make sure nothing happened. I didn't want him to get in trouble.

"Okay sweetie. Holler if you need anything," he said.

Oh I would if I needed to. But I wasn't right now. I went over to Cody's house. When I got there, I buzzed the gate, waiting a brief moment. I heard the crackle of the speakers, but then, I heard him speak.

"Is that you Amy?"

"Yeah, why?"

"Oh, I was wondering if you got my little love note I left for you. I take it that you did," he teased.

That rat bastard. What a fucking dick. I clearly didn't like the way things were at this point, and I hated that this was happening. For a long time, I simply felt like I was at a loss.

"Well I want to talk about that," I said to him.

"Fine fine. Come on in. I'm in the living room. You know where to go," he said.

Of course I did. I came here plenty of times with my dad when I was younger. It'd been a little while though, simply because we weren't friends. I wouldn't necessarily say direct enemies, but that was my dad's rival, and I hated that this was happening.

I drove in, parking the car and then walking on inside. I saw him sitting there in the living room, looking at me with a smile on his face.

"There you are," he said with a smile.

"Let's cut the bullshit. What do you want? I don't want to make this a problem for either of us. And I don't want that getting out," I said.

"Oh? That I saw you at the club, dancing and doing coke? That you're not the good little girl that you pretend to be? How cute," he said.

I gritted my teeth. I hated this guy. But he was incredibly attractive. If he wasn't such a dick, he certainly would be someone I'd consider dating. Even if it meant merging the family businesses.

"Well what do you want? I don't take kindly to this bullshit," I said to him.

"That depends. Are you ready for what I want from you?" he asked me.

I pause, d confusion present on my face.

"Well I'm here. I'm not going to leave until you tell me," I said to him.

I didn't know what the hell his endgame was. Did he want to fuck? Was there some other sort of fucked up blackmail he wanted? Did he want me to tell my dad to pull out of the business deal?

Then, he simply chuckled, looking me up and down.

"I wouldn't mind arranging something privately with you," he said.

"Well tell me. I don't want to pussyfoot around. Please," I said.

My partying days would eventually bite me in the ass, but I didn't expect this. I just didn't want my dad to get in trouble or anything either.

He then chuckled.

"It's simple. I want your ass," he said to me.

"My...ass," I told him.

"Yeah. You've got an amazing ass there Amy. I see it when you're on tv. You've had one for a while, and I of course was curious about it. If you offer that to me, I'm sure we can just put this little mess aside," he said.

Why did he want this of all things? It surprised me that something so simple, yet it made me flush crimson. He was a simple guy with a strange bargain, that's for sure.

"And that's all you want...right? You're not going to lie to me or anything?" I asked him.

In truth, I didn't think he'd be into that of all things, but then he nodded.

"Yes. We don't have to have sex in any other ways. In fact, once this is over, we can pretend to not like each other like we always did. I just think it's...proper payment for what I'm trying to get here," he said.

Payment? Did he think I was some kind of commodity for sale? It pissed me the hell off knowing this. I bit my lip though, knowing for a fact that there was no way I could argue this one.

"Fine. You win," I said to him.

His eyes widened in surprise.

"Really now?" he asked me.

"Yeah. I'm not going to fuck around or anything else. I'm just....I just want that at least. It's not much...right," he said.

179

It really wasn't all that much, but it didn't make me any less apprehensive.

"Really?"

"Yes really. Just your ass. I just want to spank it, play around with it, you know. Maybe give it a bit of a tease," he said.

I mean, I wasn't a virgin or anything, but it was a very strange thing to ask of me. but I guess so long as he doesn't tell anyone about what happened, we should be fine...right?

"Fine," I finally said.

"You mean—"

"I'll do what you asked," I muttered, flushing crimson at the idea of this.

"Very well. I figured it wasn't much to ask of you. That way we can...have a little bit of fun with this," he said to me.

"Fine," I said.

There was an awkward pause, and I wondered what exactly he'd ask of me next. I mean...would we just do this here or....

"Let's go upstairs. Follow me," he said.

His house was huge, practically a mansion. What did he have up there. I followed him, flushing at the idea of this, but when we got up there, I followed him inside.

180

"This is—"

"Ding, ding, ding, you've got it," he said.

It was a dungeon. The man had a fucking sex dungeon in his own home. I don't know why, but there was something about this which felt different, but also...I couldn't necessarily complain or anything either.

"So what now?" I asked him.

"First, I want you to put this on," he said.

"But I thought that—"

'It's to get you more comfortable. Won't affect anything," he said.

He handed me some black lingerie. It was simple, but it made me flush.

"Fine," I muttered, grabbing it and going to the bathroom. I put it in, realizing it didn't cover much. Thankfully I didn't think he was filming this, so I didn't have to worry about that embarrassment.

"Okay...just tonight. You don't have to worry about anything else once this is over," I muttered to myself.

I made my way back to the room, seeing him there, a smile curled on his face.

"Wow. You look great," he said.

"Yeah, course I do. This thing is tiny as fuck though," I told him.

"Yeah, that's the fun of it. I'm sure that it'll be fun for you to indulge in of course," he said to me.

I didn't know how to feel. Other than slightly nervous, but also a bit aroused. I mean, I could see his eyes glazing over my body, specifically towards my butt. Even though this wasn't the type of circumstances I expected, there was a thrill in this...for some odd reason.

"Get on the bed, hands and knees," he instructed.

"Okay," I said with a nervous voice. I scrambled onto the bed, realizing the sheets were very soft and plushy. Even though this was embarrassing, and bordering on blackmail, there was something exciting about this. And like...it wasn't the worst thing that could happen.

He could've just straight told my dad, or fucked him over.

So why didn't he? I had no clue, but it wasn't like I was going to ask him right now. I was just relieved that I could get him to forget about this whole mess with well...my body and all.

I laid down, my butt in the air. I felt a hand grasp it, touching it there, and then the hand squeeze it a few times. I let out a small yelp of surprise, and then I heard Cody chuckle.

"Wow, surprised by me grabbing your ass? How cute," he said.

"I wasn't surprised. Just wasn't expecting that much force you know?" I told him.?

"I know. It's kind of cute to see you like this, all flustered and turned on. Now…where were we?" he asked.

He grabbed my butt, teasing the orbs, and while I felt embarrassed to be getting pleasure from this, I couldn't help but enjoy the touch of his hands there. He continued to massage and tease my body, making me shiver and tense up, enjoying the sensation of this.

"There we go. You have such a nice and fun butt. I can't wait to give it a few little Marks here and there," he said.

"Marks?" I said, surprised by this.

"Course. I said I was going to spank it," he said.

I'd never been spanked hard before. While it did make me nervous, there was something thrilling about the way his hands hovered over there.

His hands delicately moved against the edge of my butt, little touches that made me shiver and moan, a gasp of surprise emitting from my mouth when I felt his hand move downwards, just barely teasing my pucker.

I felt so embarrassed but that embarrassment turned into surprise when I felt the smack of his hand, the arch of my hips forward, and the moan that escaped me.

"Look at you. So aroused already," he said to me.

"I…I wasn't expecting that," I told him.

"Course you weren't. you shouldn't. you should learn to relax, and embrace what I have in store for you," he teased in my ear.

What did he have in store for me? I shivered, excitement and need growing within me. I started to feel his hands rest against there slightly, and then, he hit me again.

This time, instead of feeling pain, I suddenly moaned, surprised that it felt...so good. I suddenly bucked my hips a little bit, moaning slightly.

"What's that? You're enjoying this? How surprising and lewd," he said.

"I didn't mean to make a sound. I liked it. That's all," I told him.

"I know you're enjoying this. You can lie all you want, but I can tell that you like this," he said.

It was a little bit painful, but also...I liked the fact that he was teasing my ass like this. I started to feel the hands ghost against there again, smacking me hard once more, and then another gasping moan of pleasure and desire came out of my mouth.

"Holy shit," I said, suddenly jerked to reality by how arousing and nice this was.

"There we go. Look at you, all turned on by this. How cute," he said to me.

I shivered, suddenly feeling like all eyes were on me as he grasped my ass, touching and teasing it there, making me shiver out loud, moaning slightly at the sensation of this. It was then when, moments later, he then hit me once again, another garbling sound emitting from my mouth. He hit me again and again, each spank making me suddenly cry out in pleasure, enjoying the feeling of this. It was driving me insane, making me feel like I was losing control of myself, my mind, and everything in between.

That's when I felt the smack once more, causing me to let out a small gasp, a feeling of pleasure erupting from my body, making me ache for more.

He then moved his hands back, and I let out a small sigh of need. I didn't realize how much I liked his touches until well...he did this to me. but then he chuckled.

"Miss me already?"

"Maybe I did," I replied back.

He laughed once more.

"Well I have another surprise for you before we get to the fun stuff," he said to me.

What other surprise did he have? that's when I felt something graze against my cheeks once more. It felt like a flogger, or maybe a paddle. Either way the cold leather stimulated me, making me let out a small gasp. It felt exciting, but also a bit worrisome, mostly because I had no clue what would happen to me now.

Suddenly, I felt the whack of the flogger, hitting my ass cheeks directly. I let out a small yelp of surprise, mild pain, but also pleasure. He then chuckled, doing this again and again.

"There we go. Look at you, all turned on like this. I can't believe you're so aroused just by this alone," he said to me.

"Maybe I am," I told him.

"Good. As you should be," he said to me.

He continued to paddle me, hitting me hard, and every single point of contact was turning me on, making my ass arch, and my body crave more. My fleshy ass cheeks were soon growing red, and I felt like I was getting closer to my limit.

But, with one last smack, he pulled away, lightly rubbing the cheeks. I winced slightly, realizing just how raw this felt.

"Wow, I really did do a number on your ass. I love the way that it looks right here," he said.

I let out a small moan of surprise, realizing just how raw and sore it was. But I also craved more. Even though I knew that this was just payment for his silence, there was also that thrill of course of being his, of being taken by him, and of course used like this.

I never realized how much I needed a man to just take me and use me like this.

He grasped my ass, touching it slightly, and then, he moved back.

"I think that's enough for now. You're doing great. But I can also see that you're enjoying this too. Even though I know that you're trying to hold back," he said.

I blushed. Was it really that fucking obvious? I didn't expect him to see right through this, but I guess he did.

"So what is I am?"

"Then I'm doing something right. Very right in fact," he said with a purr.

I felt the growing need for more start to take over me. I didn't expect this to come about. But then, I heard him step away from my butt, rushing towards a drawer. He got out a few things, and then, he game over, lightly massaging the cheeks with some oil.

"That should help with the soreness," he said.

I let out a gasp of surprise at the cold texture of this, but also let out a relieved sigh as I felt the contents seep in. it did help with the sting from his touches.

"Thanks. I guess," I said.

"Hey, I could just leave you like this and smack you more. But I do appreciate how well you've been taking this. Maybe you're just a fan of someone playing with your ass after all," he replied.

"Maybe," I muttered.

But the truth was, I did enjoy this far more than I let on. The little massages against the raw, red skin felt nice, but I also was a bit surprised at how easily my body reacted to this. After a little bit, he pulled back, and then, I heard him uncap something else.

"What are you going to—"

187

Then, I felt it, a finger against my pucker. I suddenly tensed up, surprised by this.

"Now Amy, you don't want to be too tense. That'll ruin the fun," he said.

I knew that I had to relax. But it was such a...a different feeling that it was hard to. He danced his fingers against my pucker, and then two fingers rubbed my clit, causing me to let out a small gasp, a moan of surprise and need.

"There we go," he said, touching me there.

I let out a low moan of surprise, amazed by how nice this was. He continued to touch, tease, and play with me, getting me turned on and ready for more. He then slowly inserted the finger inside of me, which caused me to let out a small moan of surprise and a little wince of discomfort.

It was tight. Then again, I'd never really played much with myself down there. But he slowly got the first finger into me, causing me to let out a low, guttural sound, watching with widened eyes as he began to move his fingers in and out of me, touching, teasing and playing with me. I let out a low groan of surprise as he pushed the finger in deeper, making me aroused and turned on by the sheer feeling of this.

It didn't really hurt all that much either thank fuck. At first I thought it'd hurt the entire time. But it didn't. The discomfort started to go away, and that, combined with the fingers against my entrance and clit, made things a much more enjoyable experience.

He continued this for a little while, touching and teasing me, and it was then when, after a few mere moments, he then moved himself back a teeny bit, watching me with wide eyes and a smile of excitement.

"There we go," he said to me.

"W-what now?" I said to him.

"We add another finger of course. Just relax. I'm sure you'll enjoy it," he said.

I felt a little put on the spot, but I decided to humor him, laying down there. I felt the second finger start to push into me, and I let out a small gasp of surprise and discomfort. This was much tighter. But I felt something touch against the folds of my pussy, rubbing me there, causing me to let out a small moan, suddenly feeling my whole body begin to respond to him. I let out a low sound of need, a muttering moan that made me feel turned on and excited about all of this. He continued the touches, each and every single one causing me to let out a jolt of pleasure, enjoying the feeling of this.

He continued to insert another finger into me, pushing a finger into my pussy, causing me to let out a small moan of surprise, letting my body relax and take over the pleasuring feelings that were within me. even though I was a bit nervous about this, and I didn't know what would happen to me next, I still liked this feeling. It was then when, after a few more thrusts he pushed his fingers slightly upwards, causing me to let out a small cry of surprise.

The fingers in my pussy were pushed deep, hitting a spot within me that I didn't expect to experience like ever. I suddenly started to tense up, letting out a low, guttural sound of surprise, and then, moments later I suddenly felt my whole body just tense up, enjoying the sensation of this.

Moments later, I came hard, feeling my body grow ragged with need.

He pulled the fingers out, teasing one of them against his lips. I let out a sigh of surprise, realizing how good I felt at the present moment.

"Wow," I told him.

"You good?" he asked me.

"I think so," I told him.

"AS you should be. I think it's obvious that you're enjoying this. Well, I guess it's time for the main event," he said.

Oh yeah. He was going to fuck my ass. I felt a bit nervous, but as he pulled down his pants, revealing his cock, I felt a hunger and need.

He was pretty sizable, but I wanted to imagine that I could take it. I licked my lips as I moved my body so that I was closer to him.

"What you doing?" he asked.

"Giving you this," I said.

I opened my mouth, taking his cock into my mouth, letting it slide down my throat. He suddenly let out a low groan, suddenly holding my head there, skull fucking it, enjoying the feeling of this. I let out a gasp of surprise, and it was then when he started to push the cock in deeper, and I suddenly felt my whole body tense up.

He pulled away, making me gasp in surprise as he looked into my eyes.

"Are you ready? You can get on top you know," he said.

"You sure that's a good position? I can keep it like that you know," I offered.

I'm sure that made me sound more turned on and needy than I was, but he simply smiled.

"Well if you insist…."

He then pushed me down on the bed, and then, I felt his cock at the tip of my entrance. He slowly slid in, and I suddenly felt the pain of my ass being filled up. It was a little different from my pussy, and so much fucking tighter, but I started to feel him sink all the way into me, making me shiver, tense up, and enjoying the feeling of this.

When he got all the way in, he held me there, pushing himself inside. I let out a cry as I felt him in there, both turned on and a little bit shocked by how it all fit into there.

Then, he started to move. I clung to him for a moment, but then he pushed me into the sheets., I grasped those, holding onto them as he started to move his hips, thrusting in and out, holding me there as I started to let out a series of moans, enjoying the feeling.

Every single moan, every single touch, it was all just...amazing really.

It was such a turnon that I couldn't help but enjoy the way that this felt. I held onto the sheets, feeling him sink in and out of me, pushing in deep, holding me there, causing me to realize just how turned on I was by this.

He continued his large, harsh thrusts, holding me there, but then he grabbed my hips, thrusting in deep. As he did that, I suddenly tensed up, letting out a small cry of surprise and pleasure as he continued to push into me, holding me there as he thrust himself in.

His hands moved towards my front, teasing me there, and soon I felt two fingers inside, and a finger against my clit, rubbing it and holding onto me there.

As he pushed inside I tensed up, letting out a small cry of pleasure and surprise. I couldn't believe how good this felt, how amazing this was to me. it was only moments later that he finished up, letting out a low groan, and finishing inside of me.

I felt the power of my own orgasm completely overwhelm me, and as he finished inside, he then pulled away.

I fell onto the bed, amazed but also exhausted by this. I simply laid there, and he chuckled.

"Well, you okay there? Or did I KO you?" he asked with a smile.

I turned to him, giving him a small thumbs-up.

"I enjoyed it. Don't get the wrong idea," I said.

"Really now? You enjoyed getting fucked in the ass from your rival? How scandalous! Imagine if others found out and—"

"You won't tell anyone. Because it will also backfire on you," I said, giving him a small smile.

This was different from the revelations of my partying. This of course would also reflect on him. He paused, pursing his lips and then nodding.

"Course I won't say a damn thing. I don't want to get in trouble either. But I'd be lying if I said I didn't have a good time. And you more than paid off my silence on many things of course," he said.

I flushed, realizing that I didn't have to worry. So why did I feel the urge for...more.

"I see," I said.

"Well, I guess that's it. If you want to leave you can—"

I shook my head.

"I don't want to leave. I kind of liked it Cody. I had a good time. If you wanted to do this again, I wouldn't mind it. It's not really a punishment to me," I told him.

He looked at me with surprise on his face, and then he nodded.

"Wow. I see then. I guess that settles it," he told me.

"Yeah, I'm just...I'm glad that I had a good time with all of this," I told him.

"I'm glad that you did too. I don't think this was necessarily a total punishment for you either," he said.

It wasn't. it awoke something new within me though, a series of feelings that made me excited, and I craved more. But it also made me wonder if there was something more there, if there was a chance we could do this again.

"If you wanted to do this again...I wouldn't be against it," I teased.

His eyes widened for a second, and then he nodded.

"Really now?"

"Yeah. I really enjoyed it," I told him.

He chuckled, and I wondered what was so funny to him. but then he spoke.

"I didn't expect this to happen. But you know, I wouldn't mind it either. However, we don't tell our parents about this one. Got to keep the rivalry idea in place still," he said to me.

"You're right," I said to him.

"But…I can't wait for the next time we get to have something this fun happen. I'm sure it'll be good for both of us," he said.

"I'm sure it would be too," I replied.

He leaned in, giving me a kiss, much to my surprise. At first, I wanted to tell him to fuck off, but I kind of liked it. As soon as it happened, he pulled away.

"You know, I think this is the start of something fun Amy," he said.

I grinned.

"Yeah, I think so too," I replied.

It was the start of something alright. I had no clue what would happen now, or even what we'd have to do, but I also knew for a fact that this awoke something in both of us, something neither of us were expecting, but also…I liked it. I knew that this would change the way things would go, and I didn't regret anything that had happened either.